I knew it was a risk, but I needed supplies if I was going to run successfully...

The man didn't speak but eyed me strangely while scanning my purchases. I put my backpack on the floor and packed each item carefully as he handed them to me. Finally, he was done and pointed to the total on the register. I dug the chip out of my pocket and placed it on the counter. There was just enough credit to pay for everything with a bit left over.

"PacNW chip," he said, looking at me out of the corner of his eye. "Where'd you get that? This stolen?"

"My grandmother," I said. "It was a gift. For my birthday."

"What kind of girl spends her birthday money on surplus clothes and protein bars? You a runaway? Look skinny but well fed. Healthy. Clean hands. Not like the street kids who usually come in here."

"I'm just getting s—supplies for an outdoor education trip at my s—school," I said, stammering, trying to make eye contact so he wouldn't think I was lying.

He kept looking at me sideways while he scanned the chip and handed it back to me. There was a beep and the charge was approved. I picked up my backpack and put it on. It was heavy but not as bad as it had been with Xel in it. He was facing me now and seemed to be listening to some audio on his specs.

"Yeah," he said, talking but not to me, "I think I've got your runaway right here in my shop. Last Survivor on Lincoln Street."

It's 2038, and Tara Rivers is fourteen years old, a bit rebellious, and socially awkward. Her family has recently moved to Los Angeles from the Pacific Northwest "rogue" clusters. Tara feels alone and confused. She doesn't have any friends here, except her cat, Xel, a sophisticated robot with artificial intelligence. The corporation where Tara's parents work makes an offer they can't refuse—let them put an implant in Tara's brain to "cure" her autism and make her neurotypical, or Tara's father will be prosecuted for manufactured crimes. Tara overhears her parents speaking with the doctors and decides to run away with Xel. She plans to head back to the Pacific Northwest and her grandmother, but first she must escape Los Angeles and the corporation—with all their high-tech locating devices—dodge street gangs and wild dogs, and traverse an unknown wilderness full of unimaginable dangers. Will she ever find a place where she is accepted for who and what she is, or is she doomed to be an outcast from society forever?

KUDOS for *The Place Inside the Storm*

"With a unique dystopian future and a fist-fighting robot cat, *The Place Inside the Storm* might be exactly the YA adventure you've been looking for. *The Place Inside the Storm* is a fun, fast-paced YA adventure following a brave teenage girl escaping to safety in the PacNW cluster. The book appeals to the weird in all of us, not only for its shining moral about acceptance but also for its unlikely heroes. Tune into this book even if only for Xel, the most badass robot cat in YA fiction. Author Bradley W. Wright sets us up for one hell of a ride with his premise. As Tara, Loki, and Xel begin their escape to the PacNW cluster, the reader foresees a book full of action, obstacles, growth, and plenty to pay attention to. Mix all that with easy-to-read language and clear images, and you've got yourself the makings of a pretty damn good page-turner." ~ *Independent Book Review*

"A moving and poignant story of government corruption at its worst, this chilling tale will have you on the edge of your seat all the way through." ~ *Taylor Jones, The Review Team of Taylor Jones & Regan Murphy*

"Combining science fiction, mystery, adventure, and marvelous character development, *The Place Inside the Storm* is a coming of age story that is both moving and compelling. I highly recommend it." ~ *Regan Murphy, The Review Team of Taylor Jones & Regan Murphy*

ACKNOWLEDGMENTS

I would like to thank Faith, Lauri, Arwen, and the rest of the team at Black Opal Books for all their hard work and support. I would also like to thank Shanti for reading the first draft, giving invaluable feedback, and creating the beautiful cover design.

ACKNOWLEDGMENTS

I would like to thank Faith, Lauri, Arwen, and the rest of the team at Black Opal Books for all their hard work and support. I would also like to thank Shanti for reading the first draft, giving invaluable feedback, and creating the beautiful cover design.

THE PLACE
INSIDE
THE STORM

BRADLEY W. WRIGHT

A Black Opal Books Publication

GENRE: YA/SCIENCE FICTION/ACTION-ADVENTURE/COMING OF
AGE

THE PLACE INSIDE THE STORM
Copyright © 2018 by Bradley W. Wright
Cover Design by Shanti Markstrom
All cover art copyright © 2018
All Rights Reserved
Print ISBN: 978-1-644370-43-6

First Publication: APRIL 2019

Published by Black Opal Books http://www.blackopalbooks.com

DEDICATION

For T, S, and all the G4s

CHAPTER I

The News

July 2038:

I was down at the creek behind our house when I heard my mom calling my name. A light rain was falling, but I had my gear on and didn't really mind. There was a still pool outside the main current where the water was like glass. I loved watching the drops falling on the surface, joining the stream, ripples moving out. Brown and orange leaves were floating at the edge, rocking gently. My mom called again. She sounded annoyed. She must have been yelling at me for a while.

"Be there in a second," I yelled back. Xel, my new cat was sitting next to me. The rain didn't soak into his fur. It had some kind of anti-moisture coating. The drops just beaded up and dripped down onto the wet grass. "Should we go Xel?" I asked.

He turned his head slowly and looked up at me, squeezing his eyes half shut. We ran up the hill together.

Inside the house, I took off my jacket and boots and hung them up in the mud room. There was a heating vent with a brass grill cover right under the row of hooks on the wall. I put my feet on the vent and stood for a minute, feeling the warmth through my wool socks.

"Tara, dinner!" my mom called again.

"Coming."

My mom and dad and sister Zoie were already at the table. I sat down. Minutes passed in silence as we all focused on our food. My parents were both drinking wine, which was unusual. I glanced up and watched my mom raise her glass and take a sip. She seemed tense. So did my dad. They didn't show it on their faces, but I could feel it like waves washing over me. It was overwhelming. Something was up. I looked away, took a bite of food, chewed. It felt like plastic in my mouth, tasted like cardboard. I heard my dad clear his throat.

"Tara. Zoie. We have something to tell you."

I didn't look up at him. Zoie did. I could see her out of the corner of my eye. She was waiting eagerly for the bomb, the explosion, the news. In that way we were opposites. I hated news. I hated confusion and disruption.

"I've decided to take the job at TenCat Corp," he went on. "They've offered your mother a position too."

As soon as I heard the words it was like I was falling. I could still see the table, my plate of half-eaten food, but it was like I was seeing it from far away, through the mouth of a well, and I was falling down, getting farther and farther from the opening. Black shadows and silence were hugging me and pulling me down.

CHAPTER 2

The Day Before

I dropped my backpack and sat down hard on the bed. Eyes closed, hands covering my face, I held still and let the silence and solitude calm my thoughts. After a moment, I felt Xel join me. He sprang up onto the mattress and stalked around in a slow circle, sniffing the bedspread. Done sniffing, he curled up next to me with his warm back against my thigh. I knew the warmth was from his internal fusion pack. He wasn't a real cat, but his temperature was carefully calibrated to feel like the warmth of a real cat so it fooled me most of the time, if I didn't think too much. I sat for a while longer, emptying my head, just breathing, then slowly straightened up and opened my eyes.

It had been two months since we moved to Los Angeles, but I was still getting used to the new surroundings. I spent the first fourteen years of my life in the same house so it seemed okay to take my time adjusting. Not that my parents agreed.

My new room was small, but at least it was all mine.

There was just the bed I was sitting on, a desk, a dresser, a narrow doorway leading into my own tiny bathroom. I had to admit, not sharing a bathroom with Zoie was pretty nice, but I would have happily traded the private bathroom for my life back in old Oregon in the Pacific Northwest Cluster.

My bed in our old house had a real wooden frame. It was rickety and there were at least seven coats of paint on it that chipped off and revealed colored layers like sedimentary rock. There was a spot—right where my hand hung down if I was laying on my back reading—that was completely bare from me picking at it. We left most of our furniture behind when we moved. My new bed didn't even have an underneath. It was just a raised platform that grew up out of the floor with no seam. It probably was grown actually. I remembered the TenCat relocation specialist saying something about bacterial carbon frame construction when she showed us around the building. Outside my window I could see the sun over the ocean— a flat orange disk low on the horizon. I stood up and went to the window. Our apartment was on the twenty-second floor. I looked down, way down to street level, and saw the flow of pedestrian traffic, trains, autocabs. Even from so far up, the people on the street were recognizable based on their clothes—mid- and high-level corp techs like my parents, lower-level workers mostly dressed in white jumpsuits with the logo of their corp, and students like me in school uniforms. They were all surrounded by a flashing rainbow of virtual characters and text. I focused on one, and it zoomed up toward me, a fuzzy purple bear in a little antique airplane. It was the mascot for Blinkyswig. Zoie loved Blinkyswig. She drank one of their chalky ultra-sweet protein shakes every morning for breakfast. I didn't know how she could stand it. The purple bear waved to me and flew back down toward the street.

"Disable ad content," I said and the rainbow vanished. Maybe the only good thing about moving to Los Angeles and joining TenCat Corp was getting AR specs with the ad free subscription supplied as a benefit. They weren't the newest model, but they worked. All employees and their families got them. My parents' old employer was the infrastructure branch of the PacNW Cluster Government. They didn't give much in the way of benefits. Now, whenever I wanted, I could turn on and off the juggling purple bears, dragonflies buzzing my ears, and distant T-Rex monsters holding up giant signs. Mostly, I left them off.

I watched for a minute more then flopped down, head on my pillow, and went back over my day.

It was a school day and, like usual, I spent most of it trying to be invisible. Staying invisible was the best way to have a boring day instead of an awful one. I almost managed it, but on my way home, there was a group of older girls from my programming class ahead of me. They were walking to the same train stop as me. We were a block away from our school—Playa Vista Community STEM High School which I was "very lucky to be attending" according to my mom. I closed my eyes, remembering...

ᏫᎧᏫᎧ

The light changed. I followed the group of girls and stepped up onto the raised platform that took up the middle lane of the road. A train was just pulling up. The doors slid open and I stepped on, looking around for a place to sit. Just the few minutes outside and I was already overheated and sweating through my itchy shirt. I spotted a seat a couple of rows up to my right, next to an old woman with a shopping cart that took up most of the legroom. I slid in, angling my knees out into the aisle. The train was moving slowly. I settled down into my seat and gazed out the window, checking my feed on my specs. Messages and posts scrolled by, superimposed over the buildings moving by outside: air quality alert, virus outbreak, math homework due tomorrow. We came to another stop and the doors slid open. A crowd pushed onto the train and passengers standing in the open space by the doors were forced up the aisles to accommodate the new riders.

"Nice respie."

I looked up, confused, raising a hand to my particle mask. Everybody called them respies in LA but I was still getting used to the slang. One of the girls from programming class was now standing in the aisle next to my seat. She had long, straight, black hair and somehow seemed poised and elegant despite her school uniform—the same green polo shirt and black pants I was wearing. She seemed so perfect. I squinted up at her. Her respie and her specs were both recognizably new and expensive—at least two generations newer than mine. The other three girls were also there, standing behind her. The LEDs on the front girl's respie glowed green and her voice came out sounding flat and robotic.

"I heard that it's more efficient than iteration," she said.

One of the other girls laughed, turning to face her companions, and her laughter came out with the same robotic tone.

"Sorry," I said, addressing the lead girl, confused. Then I remembered: in programming class I had made a comment about recursion being more efficient than iteration for solving the problem we were working on. The train was pulling into a stop. The girl tilted her head sideways and lifted a hand, waggling her fingers in a kind of dismissive wave as the group all turned.

"You might want to consider antiperspirant," she said, looking back over her shoulder and lifting an arm. Her companions laughed again, turning to look at each other as they walked down the aisle and exited together. I watched them go then stole a glance at my armpit. A circle of sweat was visible through my shirt...

ତ୍ରେତ୍ର

I had been teased and bullied before. It was nothing new, but it still hurt every time. Laying on my bed, I could feel the familiar tightening in my chest, anger mixed with mortification and deep lonely sadness. The incident on the train was typical. I just never seemed to be able to act like everybody else, come up with the right answer, look the right way, know what to say. Sometimes I felt like all the other people were in some kind of zoo habitat, and I was on the outside of the glass enclosure, isolated, watching and trying to figure out their rules.

I stood, walked into my bathroom, and looked at my reflection in the mirror. There was a line pressed into my skin from the respie and my hair was a frizzed out mess from the humidity outside. I sighed, picking up my hairbrush.

"I look like hell," I said to my reflection, repeating one of my mother's favorite lines.

"I think you look fine." Xel's voice was low with a little bit of rumble.

I turned and looked down. He sat on his haunches in the doorway, green eyes peering up at me. His fur was long, stippled and striped, gray and black and white. Tufts of fur curled up out of his ears. He was modeled after the North American bobcat—larger than a house cat but still much smaller than a puma or mountain lion.

"Xel. You aren't objective. You're programmed to like me no matter what."

"That may be," he replied. "However, my processing is subtly different today. The update you ran yesterday seems to have altered my perception. There is a new dimension to my thinking."

I bent down and ran my hand over his head, pushing my fingers through the soft fur. "That reminds me," I said. "I want to check in with Shen and Alberto about how their cats are doing." Back in my room, I sat down on the bed and tapped the contact on my specs. "Cybex Cat Club," I said. There was a momentary rush of blurred movement then the home page scrolled up. It was an old-fashioned web site. Shen had told me it was modeled on something called a BBS from the early days of the internet. I took a moment to scan the news feed. Nothing new.

"T-Ninety-One chat space," I said and the new page opened.

Xel was a T91 model. The newest—just released a couple of months before. My father had made a trip to Shenzhen for his final interview with TenCat and brought Xel back for me. They gave it to him as a kind of signing bonus when he took the job. T91s weren't available in North America yet and, even in Asia, very few people had them. My father had told me to keep it quiet since he wasn't really sure they were allowed to be imported. The technology had taken a massive leap between the T90 model and this one. People in the Cybex chat spaces said it was military grade artificial intelligence. Xel was just Xel to me, though. He was a good companion. He kept an eye on me, asked me how I was doing, always listened. Intellectually, I knew he was a robot cat with a neural network brain but most of the time I just thought of him as a real cat who could talk—a friend. I'd only had him for a few months but he was already a big part of my life. I turned my attention to the chat space and Shen's avatar was there. Alberto was there too.

"Tara, welcome," Shen intoned. He always spoke with a kind of deep, pretentious drawl. Shen and Alberto were sort of friends too but not the kind I would ever meet for real, in person.

"Hello, Shen," I answered. "Hi, Alberto."

"Hi, Tara."

"How are your cats?" I asked, jumping straight to business.

"We were just talking about that," Alberto answered. "Jashi started acting funny after the update. She was saying words in the wrong order. Not making sense—"

"The same thing happened with Bao," Shen broke in. "I had to roll back the update. Alberto did too. But Xel is okay?"

"Yeah—seems to be," I answered, running my hand through his fur and feeling his body rumble with a low purr. "He said something about perceiving things differently. I don't know what that means. I didn't use the same mod as you two, though. I modded the mod."

"What did you change?" Alberto asked.

Soon we were into a deep discussion of the T91 firmware code. Xel curled next to me on the bed, one ear turned my way as if he was listening in. I had been hacking since I was old enough to read and write. My parents were both programmers. It was the natural language and activity of our family. Except for Zoie—my little sister didn't want anything to do with writing code. Sometimes I wondered whether I really cared about it myself. Maybe I just did it because it was expected, because I had never really tried anything else. I was good at it though. I knew that. My solution to the problem in programming class earlier had been much better than the one in the book—simpler and more elegant. It didn't matter though. I was a freshman in a junior level class. They weren't going to listen to anything I had to say.

I ended up transmitting my version of the firmware to Alberto and Shen so they could try it out and made a plan to speak with them the next day so we could compare notes. With a quick command, I hopped then over to Dazzled.

Rosie, my best friend from Oregon, was online. I browsed through her recent feed. There were posts about parties, class trips, a recent outdoor education field trip. Looking at her posts I found myself yearning for home. Not this place, this wasn't home. Yes, it was colder there, and it rained all the time, and everybody was poor, but it was my real home. PacNW was poor, a rogue cluster with no support from the federal government. Before we moved, my parents were both programmers for the cluster government. My father complained all the time about having to keep the power and sewage treatment plants running with patches on top of patches, both physical and digital. He had jumped at the chance to move south, and my mother had been excited about it too. TenCat Corporation was a step up for both of them. They had explained it all, but it still felt like a step back for me. It had never been easy to make friends. The few I had were precious. Suddenly, Rosie's avatar popped up.

"Tara! How are you?"

I felt the tears I had held back earlier begin to roll down my cheeks. "I'm okay," I answered but my voice was thick with the sob I was holding in.

"You don't sound okay."

"I miss you," I said. "LA sucks."

ຕຽຕ

I spent half an hour talking to Rosie, calming down and telling her about the new school, the building where we lived, the few trips we had made on weekends to museums and shopping. Eventually, her mom came home and she had to go. I said goodbye, feeling better but still not great, then settled back and just lay there on my bed, thinking. Leaving the PacNW cluster was not like a normal move. It would be hard to go back. The federal government was fine with people moving out, especially skilled workers.

They didn't allow migration back into rogue clusters like PacNW though. I would probably never see Rosie again unless she decided to go to college somewhere outside PacNW and her parents actually let her go. I was picturing us reuniting freshman year of college when a message marked urgent popped up, pulsing silently. I considered ignoring it but decided it might be from my mom, asking me to pick Zoie up or something.

"Open new," I said and the text zoomed in. It was a string of numbers, a line break, then another string of numbers. Below that it said:

freedom and safety

There was nothing else to the message. I looked at the sender line and it just said *anonymous*. I had never seen that before. I didn't even know it was possible. I looked back at the numbers. They were GPS coordinates I realized suddenly. Weird. Maybe it was some kind of joke or marketing campaign.

"Tara?" my mother's voice said. "I'm home. Are you in your room?"

"Close message. Archive," I said and the message faded away. "In here," I called.

I heard footsteps then my mother's head appeared,

leaning into the doorway. She kept her hair short since the move. I was still getting used to it.

"Resting?"

"Yeah."

"Did you do your homework already?"

"I only have one assignment. I'll do it after dinner."

"Okay. You all right? Ava told me you covered your biosensor." Her voice was distracted, and I could see that she was looking at something in her feed. Ava was the house computer. I could never bring myself to call the computer by name. I called Xel by his name, but that was different. I glanced at the woven metal tube on my wrist. There was just a bit of sun left above the horizon and the steel thread gleamed in the light from the window, throwing off tiny rainbows. Rosie gave it to me before I left. All minors in the federalist clusters were required to have biosensors. It was like a tattoo but with functional circuitry. I liked to cover mine up because otherwise the house computer was always telling me my blood sugar level was low or I was dehydrated.

"Fine. I just want to rest until dinner." I answered.

Zoie's head and torso appeared then, leaning around the doorway too. She was still wearing her black leotard from dance class.

"Lazy sister," she said, "Always sleeping."

"Shut up, Zoie!" I sat up. "Mom, make her go away."

"Okay, let's go," my mom said, disappearing from the doorway.

Zoie's face lingered for a moment, sticking her tongue out at me, then she was jerked away with a look of surprise.

I flopped back down on the bed and closed my eyes. Something felt weird about the way my mother had been acting the last couple of days. She wasn't normally distracted. We didn't spend a lot of time talking to each other but, when we did talk, she was usually laser focused like she was with everything else she did.

My father, on the other hand, was always distracted—reading something in his feed or thinking about some problem he was working on. Nothing new there.

I fidgeted and thrashed, unable to get comfortable.

"Is there something wrong, Tara?" Xel asked from the foot of the bed where he was curled up.

I knew he wasn't really sleeping. He didn't sleep. But it was part of his programming to act like a real cat. So, he spent a lot of time laying on my bed with his eyes closed.

"I don't know what's up with my mom, Xel. She never used to be too busy to talk to me. It's almost like there's something she doesn't want to talk about. Like she's avoiding having a conversation."

"Interesting," Xel replied. "In western psychological theory, there is a concept known as avoidance behavior or avoidance coping. It is related to anxiety. Perhaps your mother feels anxious about having forced you to move and leave behind your friends. Maybe she is avoiding speaking with you so she doesn't have to discuss it."

I eyed Xel. He had never offered this kind of opinion before. "That sounds really possible, Xel. I hadn't thought about it that way," I answered.

He looked back at me, blinking his eyes slowly.

"Dinner is ready. Please come to the dining room." It was the house computer. I sat up and swung my legs over the side of the bed.

"I'll be back in a while, Xel," I said, patting his head. "You stay here. Mom doesn't like it when you're in the dining room."

Xel squeezed his eyes closed again, nodded, and cocked his head to the side, watching me go.

ᘒᘓᘒ

"The problem is that the concentration of the drop-
lets is suboptimal…"

My mother and father were discussing a project at
work. My father was on a team working to make Ten-
Cat's cloud brightening technology more efficient. I
didn't understand it, mainly because my father never
stopped to explain. I looked over at Zoie and saw that she
was zoned out, staring at something virtual happening
behind her specs. I zoned out too, staring at my plate.
Half my dinner was still there, uneaten. The idea of putting another bite in my mouth made me feel nauseous. It
was instafood. All the right nutrients were there in the
right amounts, but it didn't taste very good. You had to
eat it without thinking about what you were putting in
your mouth and swallowing. If you concentrated on the
food or the flavor at all, it became difficult to continue.
My father used to cook real food sometimes when I was
younger. He liked to try complicated recipes. My mother
never cooked. Now, we ate instafood pretty much all the
time, except on the rare occasions when we went out to
eat. I got up, scraped the rest of my food into the composter, and put my plate in the washer.

"I'm going to do my homework," I said.

My father didn't look up, just nodded and kept talking. Zoie didn't look up either. She was smiling at something, eyes distant. My mother turned her head, giving me
a strange look. I couldn't tell what it meant so I shrugged
and continued on out of the dining room. Back in my
room I flopped down next to Xel.

"How was dinner," he asked.

"Same as always," I answered. "More weird vibes
from my mom."

"Maybe you should ask her about it directly when you get a chance."

"That's probably good advice," I said, thinking about my mom's face when I got up from the table. "I will."

I spent the next hour working on my homework. I had to write a two page biography of an important scientist. That was all the info the assignment gave. Since starting at PVCSTEM I had noticed that the teachers gave really vague assignments. I didn't do well with vague so I always asked Xel to help.

He suggested Margaret Hamilton—a computer scientist who worked on the Apollo space program—and gave me a possible outline. I researched her for a while then quickly stitched all my notes together into a paper. It was eighty percent done. I could finish it tomorrow. I didn't feel like doing any more. I was in the middle of a good book—an old SciFi novel from the nineteen-seventies. I wanted to just go to bed, read for a while, and then fall asleep.

"Done with your homework?" It was my mother, poking her head around the door again.

"Yes. I'm going to get ready for bed."

"Okay. Remember, I'm picking you up from school at eleven-thirty for your doctor appointment tomorrow."

I looked at her, puzzled. I didn't remember her saying anything about the appointment before. "What doctor appointment?"

"It's just a check-up."

"But I just had a check-up before we moved."

"They weren't able to transfer your medical records. You need to see your new doctor. Be at the front desk at eleven thirty, okay?" She was already walking away.

"Mom?" I called after her but she didn't answer. I turned to Xel. "Do you see what I mean? She's acting weird."

He looked toward the door. "You should go talk to her, Tara."

"I don't want to right now. I'm going to get ready for bed." First, though, I pulled up my calendar and checked the upcoming events. There it was—sandwiched between a quiz in math class and a notification that my essay was due by three p.m.—an appointment with someone named Dr. Kimberly Gutierrez.

I couldn't figure out how I had missed it before. I took off my specs, dropped them on the desk next to my bed, and got up. "The appointment is there, Xel. Am I losing my mind?"

"It is common for human adolescents to go through a period of absent mindedness and distraction at your age. There are hormonal effects—"

"Adolescent!" I said, cutting him off. "Did you just call me an adolescent?"

Xel blinked at me. "Technically, the age of—" he began, but I cut him off again.

"Fine. I don't want to be called an adolescent, though. Can you just say teenager?"

"Very well." He seemed taken aback, as much as it was possible for a cat to express something like that, anyway. "I apologize if the term distressed you."

"I'm sorry for yelling, Xel. It just seems so clinical."

"I understand."

"Okay. I'm going to brush my teeth."

☙❧

Ten minutes later I crawled under the covers. Xel was curled at the foot of the bed, eyes closed, purring. I put on my specs and opened the book I was reading. The page scrolled up and I picked up where I had left off.

The unforetold, the unproven,
that is what life is based on...

It was a line of dialogue, one character speaking to another. I thought about that for a moment. It seemed true but it also seemed to have nothing to do with my life. Every day was the same for me, everything predictable. Something unforetold might be nice but I wasn't going to hold my breath. I shrugged and continued reading.

CHAPTER 3

Escape

I stepped off the train at McConnell and shuffled along with the crowd, crossing the street and heading toward PVCSTEM. Luckily, the air was clear and there were no pathogen alerts so I was free of my respie at least until the afternoon.

The day was warm and muggy already. The heat made the stiff fabric of my school uniform feel hot and rough against my skin. My mom said I would get used to it before long and then I wouldn't want to live anywhere else.

She was from California back when it was still called that, before the plagues and floods and the reorganization. So was my father. Neither of them had ever gotten used to the cold and rain in PacNW so I didn't know how they could say I would get used to the heat.

"Tara, honey. Good morning." Renata, the security guard, waved me in and squeezed my shoulder as I passed through the doors.

"Good morning," I said, turning to smile back at her

as I followed the crowd of other students through the air-lock.

Inside, I pulled up my schedule on my specs and scanned it while making my way to my locker. Math first period, Biology second period, then meet my mother downstairs to go to my appointment. Lovely.

☙❧☙

"Tara, your turn."

I looked up from my tablet where I was carefully coloring the parts of a cell. I had chosen lime green for the cytoplasm. I thought it looked nice but my lab partner Jonas did not seem impressed. He was a new student too—six inches shorter than me with perpetually greasy looking hair plastered to his forehead. He was pointing to the microscope. There was only five minutes left but I tapped a button on my screen anyway and the yellowish cluster of cells under the microscope lens faded in. I stared at the screen for a while, focusing on different parts. Zooming in and out and making notes.

"Time to pack up, class. Put your scopes on the shelf. Wipe down your tables." Mr. Bhatia's deep voice reverberated through the lab. Unlike most of the other teachers at PVCSTEM, Mr. Bhatia didn't seem to like being called by his first name. Everybody called him Mr. B. Jonas took the microscope to the shelf while I wiped down the table. The wipes had a nasty, overwhelming citrus smell that made my head hurt so I touched it as little as possible and carried it to the garbage on the end of my tablet stylus. Mr. B dismissed us with a wave, barely looking up from his desk where he was fiddling with a broken piece of equipment.

"Bye, Tara." Jonas was right behind me in the crowd of students squeezing out of the classroom.

"Bye, Jonas," I replied over my shoulder.

I didn't want to get into a conversation with him. He was into some sort of VR game and talked about it incessantly if you got him started. I understood. I could be obsessive about things and bad at conversation too. Right after we moved, we went out to dinner with a couple of my parents' new coworkers. They had a daughter my age who went to a different school. I spent the entire meal telling her about Xel and didn't realize she was totally bored until my mother mentioned it later. That wasn't a good conversation. Jonas was all right. I didn't feel like humoring him right then though so I hurried off, walking fast and not looking back.

I stopped by my locker quickly then headed downstairs. My mother was already there in the lobby waiting. She was seated on the bench by the door, her back straight as the wall behind her. Her clothes were always crisp and perfect looking.

She stood up when she saw me. "Let's hurry. I already signed you out."

An autocab was parked at the curb outside and the doors clicked open as we approached. I climbed in first and my mother followed.

"Where would you like to go today?" The car computer had a pleasant, female voice with a slight British accent.

My mother gave the address of the TenCat Family Clinic and the autocab immediately pulled away from the curb, inserting itself cleanly into the flow of traffic.

"Under current traffic conditions, your trip should take approximately twenty-three minutes."

"Great," my mother replied, looking at the clock on the dashboard. "We should be there right on time." She tapped the contact on her specs and switched to looking at something in her feed. I stared out the window, watch-

ing the scenery. She was giving quiet voice commands, dictating responses to work-related messages. I felt like I should follow Xel's advice and try talking to her but there was a tightness in my throat that stopped me from speaking. I imagined various ways to start the conversation but nothing seemed right. Instead, I just kept watching the buildings pass by outside. So many of the storefront windows were covered—places that used to sell clothing, jewelry, parts for old-fashioned cars you operated yourself. They still had a few manually operated cars back in PacNW but they were outlawed years ago in the CoastSW cluster. Outside of Playa Vista the streets were dusty and barren. The few trees still standing were dead. The few people on the sidewalks and the train platforms moved slowly or grouped themselves in patches of shade. Soon though we reached the outskirts of Santa Monica and things began to look nicer. There were office buildings with palm trees and grass outside, people strolling the sidewalks with young children, restaurants with outdoor seating.

The autocab turned into a driveway and headed down a ramp into a massive garage. There were a couple of other cars ahead of us in the drop off lane. We inched forward while my mother continued to work. Finally, we came to a standstill and the curbside door opened silently.

"Thank you for riding. Your total is forty-three dollars, seventy-six cents charged to your account."

The autocab's computer seemed to have an almost impatient tone but I knew I must be imagining it. My mother tapped her specs and followed me out, pointing to a set of glass doors that slid open as we approached. Inside was a small lobby with two elevators. While we waited side by side for the elevator I fidgeted, feeling a pressure building inside me. The feeling welled up, rising through me until I suddenly found myself speaking.

"Mom. I feel like you aren't talking to me. Like you're avoiding talking to me. There's something you're holding back."

She turned her head, her mouth open. "Tara. I—"

"You don't have to say anything. It's okay. It just came out."

The elevator doors slid open and I strode inside then turned and leaned against the wall, wrapping my arms around myself.

"We'll talk after your appointment," she said.

I didn't look at her. I just nodded and continued staring at the floor. I felt raw. Expressing emotion wasn't something we did much in my family. Even just the few words I had spoken seemed somehow over the top. I knew intellectually that it wasn't weird for parents and kids to talk about important things. I had seen Rosie do it with her mom. They were always hugging and having long talks. My parents were just different, self-contained.

After checking in, we sat awkwardly and waited. A couple of other parents were there waiting with their kids. One of the kids was about four years old. He had straight, thick blond hair in a bowl cut and was running around the waiting room pretending to be an airplane. He made a low, rumbling engine noise and occasional high pitched beeps—clearly in his own world. I watched him race around until, finally, a woman poked her head out of a door and called my name. She led us down a soft carpeted hallway with regularly spaced office doors on the right and occasional branching hallways to the left. I didn't see any exam rooms. Just offices with desks and chairs. I was about to ask if we were in the right place when she stopped abruptly and gestured us into one of the offices—identical to the others we had passed. My mother stepped in and I followed. The woman entered after us and held out her hand to me.

"Good afternoon, Tara. I'm Dr. Gutierrez."

She was a tall woman, taller than me, with black hair in a braid. She stooped as she spoke, flexing her knees, getting her face close to mine, and trying to make eye contact. It drove me crazy when adults did that. I hated making eye contact with people—it just felt weird and overly intimate. Just thinking about it made me flinch and freeze up. I leaned away and looked over at my mother. She had already seated herself facing the desk, hands in her lap and gaze fixed straight ahead.

"I thought I was here for a checkup," I said, staring at the side of her face. She was still avoiding looking back at me.

"You are, Tara," Dr. Gutierrez said, seating herself behind the desk. "A different kind of checkup, though. We're just going to talk for a while. I want to find out about your emotional health."

"A psychologist? Again?" I turned to my mother. "Mom. You told me this was a regular checkup! You lied to me." The situation was outrageous. My parents had taken me to see a psychologist once before, when I was seven. It had not gone well, and they told me I didn't have to go back. Now this.

"Your parents are worried about you, Tara. They want you to make friends and be happy. We're going to just chat for a while, get to know each other. I'm going to ask your mother to leave now so we can speak without any reservations."

I sat there, furiously moving my gaze back and forth between the two of them while Dr. Gutierrez spoke. My heart was racing and blood was pounding in my ears.

My mother stood up and finally looked at me. "Tara, please give Dr. Gutierrez a chance. We just want to see if there is anything we can do to help you be happier. I'm sorry I lied to you, but you wouldn't have come otherwise." She bent down and kissed the top of my head then left the room quickly, closing the door behind her. The spot where she had kissed me felt warm. It wasn't a normal gesture.

I turned to the doctor. "Fine. Tell me what you want me to say," I spat out, folding my arms over my chest.

She smiled back at me. It seemed like an insincere smile. Maybe fake. Her face was bent into the plains and shapes I associated with a smile but I wasn't getting a happy relaxed vibe from her. She seemed tense actually and maybe a little afraid. Feeling her emotions made me tense and afraid.

"I don't *want* you to say anything, Tara. I just want to ask you some questions. I would appreciate it if you would answer truthfully. So we can help you."

It seemed pretty obvious that I wasn't getting out of there without doing some talking so I nodded. "Okay. Fine. Ask."

She nodded, pulled up something on her specs, then turned her eyes back to me. "Let's begin with this. I'm going to make some statements and I want you to reply or react."

I nodded. "Okay."

"Wow, it's really hot in here."

I waited for her to continue but she didn't say anything else. "Is a response required?" I asked. "You just said it's hot."

"A pro-social reaction would be to agree and then ask if we could adjust the thermostat."

I nodded again, feeling dumb. What was she getting at?

She spent almost an hour questioning me and taking notes. She made more weird statements, asked a lot of questions about my childhood, my friends back in PacNW, my relationship with my parents and my sister, my hobbies and interests. Finally, she smiled her fake smile again and sat back in her chair. "That's enough for now, Tara. Thank you for answering my questions. Your parents are in the office next door. I'm going to go meet with them, and we'll be back for you soon. Please wait here." She stood up.

"Wait. My dad is there too? What's he doing here?"

"Just standard procedure, Tara. We like to speak with both parents when possible."

I sat back and watched her leave. She closed the door behind her, and I heard a lock click. Did she just lock me in? I wondered. The whole situation was starting to freak me out. Why was my father there? He never took time off work. I put my ear to the wall but could only hear heavily muffled voices, not loud or clear enough to make out words. There was an intercom on the wall. I recognized the brand because it was the same as the ones in the classrooms at my old school. This one looked similar but newer. The maintenance man at my old school was not great with any kind of digital technology so he was always asking Ms. Jenkins, my technology teacher, to help out. The system needed to be reprogrammed because they had changed the numbering of the classrooms and Ms. Jenkins handed off the project to me and two other kids in the class. I knew, based on that experience, that you could call out to or listen in on any other intercom in the system if you knew the number and the passcode. I had seen the number of Dr. Gutierrez's office on our way in. It was 512. So, the office next door was probably either 510 or 514, assuming odd numbers were on one side of the hallway and even on the other. The default passcode for the system at my old school was 9999. People never bothered to change default passwords. My father complained about it all the time. I decided to risk it. Holding my breath I punched 9999*510 into the keypad then pressed the listen button. A tired sounding voice droned out of the speaker. The default passcode worked!

"Charlie, I appreciate your knowledge of airplanes but would you please answer the question I asked?" This was followed by a vrooming engine sound and a high-pitched beep. It was the boy from the waiting room. It had to be the wrong office. "Give 'em hell, Charlie," I whispered as I pressed the button to break the connection. Next I tried 9999*514. There was silence for a moment, then I jumped at the sound of my father's voice coming clearly through the speaker.

"Are you sure about this diagnosis? I know she has trouble making friends, and she's not great in social situations, but she's not so much different from me in that way."

"We are very sure, Mr. Rivers." It was a man's voice I hadn't heard before.

Then Dr. Gutierrez began speaking. "Yes. We would not be having this conversation otherwise. We have reviewed the footage of Tara at school, interacting with her teachers and classmates. We have reviewed her online social interactions and presence. We have data from your interviews and now from speaking with Tara herself. We feel very strongly that the diagnosis is accurate. If we had seen her when she was younger, we could have caught it earlier but, of course, you were in the Pacific Northwest cluster. Here, she would have had a full genetic workup early on. We would have known. Medical care in the rogue clusters is spotty."

They had been watching me? Secretly recording my interactions with other people? What the hell was going on? I had a sick feeling in my stomach, and my heart was beating rapidly.

"And the treatment you are suggesting—please explain again," my mother asked.

"It's quite simple. We do a very small operation. A tiny neural implant is placed just inside the skull. This implant can read electrical activity and redirect suboptimal responses to more desired outcomes."

"It seems so barbaric."

"I assure you it is not. This is a proven treatment. It would not have been available to you before, but now that you are here and now that you are valued members of the TenCat family, we can help you with this sort of issue. We want your daughter to be able to fit into the culture of our corporation. We want her to be able to go to a good college, succeed, build a network of peers, and become a valued member of TenCat in her own right."

"But won't it...change her? Change her personality?" my mother asked.

"She will still be your daughter. Slowly, she will become more pro-social. She will seek out healthy, normal relationships. She will make eye contact. She will get better at understanding social cues. Her theory of mind or ability to understand how other people are feeling will improve. Yes, she may seem different, but it will help her be more adjusted and normal."

I felt an icy chill creep down my spine as Dr. Gutierrez spoke. They wanted to put a computer chip in my head? I already had one in my arm. I guessed that was just the first step. Now they wanted to control my mind instead of just keeping tabs on my hydration and blood sugar levels. Why were my parents just sitting there? Why weren't they saying no, walking out, slamming the door?

"What if we say no?" my father asked, sounding dismayed.

"The issue with the T-Ninety-One cat is serious. You did bring the cat with you?" It was the man speaking again.

"Yes, Mr. Rivers brought it," Dr. Gutierrez said. "It's in the conference room next door, powered down."

"Good," the man responded. "The authorities are willing to let it go as long as you give your consent to this treatment. Of course, the cat will have to be factory reset. The modifications your daughter made are unorthodox and possibly dangerous. She removed certain security measures meant to keep the cat from achieving complex emotional states. She actually transmitted the hacked firmware to two other T-Ninety-One owners. This therapy will make your daughter more positively aligned with social expectations. Of course, we will have to monitor her activities on an ongoing basis, but I do not think we will have to worry about her altering the firmware on her cat again once we start. She will be more interested in making friends and engaging in social activities."

The chill continued to grow, freezing me in place. I was immobilized with panic. This was not good. They wanted to control my brain, change how I thought. Reset Xel so he wouldn't even recognize me. Make me into a zombie with a computer implanted in my head. They wanted me to become a different person. Yes, I had always had trouble socializing. I had trouble caring about the stuff regular kids were into. I liked computer programming and old science fiction books. But my friend Rosie back home was proof that I wasn't a total loser, wasn't she? I just needed to meet people who were on my wavelength. I didn't want to be like the regular kids. I liked who I was, even if I was a little weird.

I went to the door and tried the handle. It was locked. There was a keypad, but my chance of somehow guessing the code was pretty dismal. I needed to get out. I could still hear them speaking, talking about the operation, the recovery time, how much school I would have to miss. I went to the window. It was sealed. My panic was growing. I couldn't let them do it to me. I would run away. Making the decision calmed me. I felt a fierce determination take over my body, guiding my actions. They would not catch me. Looking up, I saw a louvered vent in the ceiling. It looked like it covered an air duct for heating and cooling. Quickly, I pulled a chair over, stood on it, worked my fingers into the spaces between louvers, and yanked. The vent cover came free easily and hinged open, hanging to the side. Above it was a duct that looked large enough for me to climb into. I jumped down, grabbed my school backpack, quickly emptied out everything I wouldn't need, then shoved it up into the vent. The next part would be tricky. I was not athletic or graceful. My body often felt completely out of phase with my brain. I didn't have any other option at the moment, though, so I wrapped my fingers over the edge of the duct then jumped and pulled with my arms at the same time. Surprisingly, I managed to get my upper body into the duct then wriggle forward until I could pull my legs in too. It was tight, but I fit. I gave silent thanks for my skinniness. Most of the time I thought it made me look awkward, but it was a benefit in this situation. Wriggling back, I reached down and pulled the vent cover up, clicking it into place. Hopefully, it would take a while for them to realize how I had gotten out of the office. Now I had a decision to make. Try to get past where my parents and the doctors were talking so I could rescue Xel, or go the other way? Option two would get me out faster and give me a better chance of escaping, but I knew what I had to do.

It was very warm and dark up in the duct. It felt almost peaceful in a way. I could see light up ahead where the vent for the next office was. Farther on, I could see another patch of light that must be the vent for the conference room Dr. Gutierrez had mentioned. That was where I needed to get to, but I had to be silent. I wormed my way forward, holding my backpack up with my arms out in front of me so it wouldn't drag on the metal of the duct. My progress was slow but I made it to the vent. I could see the top of my father's head below. They were still talking.

"…gross motor skills may also improve."

"Yes, she has always been a little clumsy."

Clumsy! It was true, but I wasn't going to let anything stop me. I kept moving, praying that they wouldn't look up or hear me passing by. With a sigh of relief, I made it to the next vent. I pushed the vent cover, and it swung down on its hinge. Below, I could see an expanse of dark wood. It was a long table. Carefully, I eased my legs through the opening. The thought of dropping blindly down terrified me but I didn't have any other options so I closed my eyes, gritted my teeth, and let myself slide out of the duct, holding my backpack to my chest. My feet hit the table below almost immediately, and I stumbled but kept my footing, dropping down to one knee. For a moment I just crouched there, eyes still closed. When I finally opened my eyes, I saw chairs around the table, a window looking out over a busy street, and, in the corner, a wooden box. I knew the box. I recognized the writing on the side in big red Chinese characters. It was the box Xel came in. My father must have gotten it out of my closet and packed Xel into it. I still couldn't believe it. I closed the vent cover, scrambled off the table, and opened the box. He was there, laying on his side, eyes closed. I gasped. I knew he wasn't dead. He was just powered down. But it was still hard to see him like that. I ran a hand over his head.

"Let's get out of here," I said and lifted him out of the box.

Carefully, I lowered him into my backpack. He was heavy—maybe twenty-five or thirty pounds. He fit into the backpack just barely. Luckily, it was a gym day at school so I had my large bag. My gym clothes and sneakers were now scattered on the chair in Dr. Gutierrez's office. I zipped the pack up, careful not to catch Xel's whiskers. With a start, I realized I wouldn't be going back to PVCSTEM that day. Maybe not ever. No more gym class. I had to escape first, though. Pulling the backpack on wasn't easy, but I managed. Carrying it felt like giving my sister Zoie a piggy back ride.

The conference room door wasn't locked. I opened it a crack and looked out. The hallway was empty. Across from the door was another hallway. Far away at the end, I saw a red EXIT sign. *Now or never*, I decided and headed for the sign at a brisk walk. When I was halfway down the corridor, a door opened ahead of me and a tall man in a white lab coat came out. I kept walking, keeping my head down, feeling pricks of nervous sweat on my forehead.

"Are you lost?"

I looked up, forcing myself to meet his eyes. "Yes—looking for the bathroom." *Crap! What a stupid thing to say! What if he points me back in the other direction?*

"Keep going this way. It's on the left just before you get to the end of the hallway." He headed off up the corridor, not giving me another look.

I hurried off, too. When I got to the end, I looked back but he was out of sight. Just then an urgent message popped up on my specs. I swiped it away and turned my attention to the door. It was an emergency exit, but it didn't appear to have an alarm, so I pushed through and found myself in a stairwell. I paused for a minute, thinking. If I ran for it now, they would find me in no time. I would be out on the sidewalk in Santa Monica in broad daylight. It would be better to find somewhere to hide in the hospital building and then escape at night. I longed to run down the stairs, burst through the doors at the bottom, and make a break for it. I had to force myself to be logical, though. I turned and headed up the steps.

After two flights, I reached a landing and a metal door. There was a small window in the door looking out onto the roof of the building. Twenty feet away, through a haze of heat, I saw what looked like a maintenance room. Maybe for access to elevator systems or something else. It was worth a try, so I pushed the door open and stepped out onto the roof. The sun beat down on my head as I hurried across. When I reached the door, I grasped the handle, said a little prayer, and turned it. The handle offered no resistance and the door swung open, revealing a shadowy room with little spots of green and red where LEDs glowed on instrument panels. I stepped inside quickly and closed the door behind me. This place would have to do. It would be my refuge while I waited for nightfall.

CHAPTER 4

Running

The first thing I did was shut off the data connection on my specs. Next, I carefully lowered my backpack to the floor and, fumbling in the dark, found the woven metal tube, and yanked it on over my biosensor. Now they wouldn't be able to track me. Xel's fur felt soft and cool to the touch as I reached into the pack again. What did the man say about my firmware mod? It was dangerous somehow? *Never mind*, I thought and pushed it out of my head. I couldn't think about Xel right now. I had to find out where I was and make a plan. My fingers closed on a little LED keychain flashlight I always keep in my pack.

As I pulled it out and turned it in my palm, I remembered the day I got it. It was one of the few nice days we had spent as a family since the move. We had all gone to the Science Museum to see an exhibit about life in the Mars colony. Afterward, we had stopped in the gift shop, and I had chosen the flashlight. Pushing the memory from my mind, I turned it on and surveyed the room.

The walls and floor were bare concrete. On the wall opposite the door were several large metal boxes with pipes and conduit running in and out of them. They looked like racks for computer or electrical equipment. There was a loud hum in the room coming from an AC unit on the ceiling. It was annoying but better than the sweltering heat outside. Next to the door was a metal cabinet taller than me.

I pulled the door open. It was empty except for a couple of pairs of work gloves on an upper shelf and a gallon can of paint. It would be a good place to hide in case anybody came looking. I quickly lifted the shelves out and put them on top of the cabinet. With my legs tucked up, backpack between my knees, I sat down inside and pulled the door most of the way closed.

Sitting there in the dark, my body began to relax, I started to shiver, and an overpowering loneliness crept up from my stomach. A great sob convulsed my chest and tears stung my eyes. What the hell was I doing? Was I really running away? I thought about my parents and the doctors. Was I losing my mind? The tears flowed, and my nose ran. I shook my head. No, I wasn't. I knew what I heard them say.

I couldn't let them do that to me. I couldn't let them put a computer in my head that would change me, control me. They could make me do anything, act any way they wanted. I lifted a hand and felt the place on the crown of my head where my mother had kissed me. She never did that. Thinking about her made the sadness and fear even worse. I hunched forward as the sobs rolled through me, drawing ragged breaths. Would I ever see them again? My parents and my sister? If I managed to get away, where would I go? What would I do? I would have to figure that out later. For now, if I was going to get away,

I had to be smart and brave and worry about the present, not the future.

I didn't know how long it took but finally the sobbing lessened and the tears stopped. After that, I just sat still in the dark and waited. I thought about my whole life—the life left behind when we moved. It wasn't bad. I was fine before. I could be again. They didn't give me time to adjust. Why did the doctors think I needed to be fixed? I thought about the happiest times in my life. It came to me then that I was happiest when I was being myself, when I was free to be myself. Most of the time I hid. I was used to hiding my true self. I was good at it. When you're a weirdo, you get used to trying not to be seen or heard. Quiet is safe. The less people notice you the better. Sometimes, though, when I was with Rosie, or by myself, or just hanging out with my father programming, not talking, I could let my guard down and just exist. Those were the best times.

A fumbling at the door to the room brought me out of my daze, and I quickly pulled the cabinet shut, holding my breath, heart pounding. I heard the door swing open. Through the small cracks around the edges of the cabinet I saw light—a flashlight beam swinging around the room. A voice suddenly cut through the silence but it sounded like it was coming from a speaker.

"Report in. Any sign of the girl? Over." This was followed by a short pause while the light continued to move around the walls, the corners. I heard two steps, then the cabinet door was pulled open. I sat there, frozen, looking up. The flashlight beam blinded me for a moment then swung up, pointing at the ceiling. I saw a middle aged man, probably my father's age, looking down at me. He was dressed all in black. He slowly raised has hand and tapped the contact on his specs, not taking his eyes off me.

"Officer Huang reporting. Checking the roof. Nothing yet. Over."

"Finish searching the roof then return to the security office. Over."

"Copy that. Over." He lowered his hand, still watching me. "Be careful," he said, "Best time to get away is early morning. I wouldn't let them do that to me either, or my daughter. Good luck."

"Thank you," I whispered, but the door was already banging closed.

He was gone. Slowly, I relaxed. It took a few minutes for me to process what had happened. I could hardly believe he hadn't turned me in. It felt like a confirmation that I was doing the right thing, that they were misguided, that what they wanted to do to me was wrong. Silently, I thanked him again, sending out my energy, hoping he would catch it.

I needed to hide out until early morning—he said it would be the best time to get away and there was no reason to doubt him. It wasn't going to be easy. Resigning myself to a long wait, I sat back and wiggled around into a more comfortable position. I realized I was hungry so I searched in my backpack. Again I felt Xel's compact body. Should I wake him? I wondered. How would he react? Would he tell me to go home? What would he do if I refused? He was loyal to me, but there might be some override. He might be required by his programming to turn me in. I could use his help and guidance. Vast amounts of knowledge were saved in his memory. I needed a friend too. I couldn't risk it just then, though. I would have to wait and wake him up later. I continued digging and found an old protein bar at the bottom of the pack. It was all the food I had so I ate it slowly, savoring every bite. After I finished the bar, I leaned back and pulled up the book I was reading on my specs. It felt weird to be sitting there in a metal cabinet, in a concrete room, on the roof of a hospital, reading a book while people searched for me down below. I needed to take my mind off the situation, though, and reading was a good way to do that. Reading had always been my escape.

೧ఌ೧ఌ

At five a.m., I decided it was time. I had actually slept for a few hours, curled up uncomfortably in the cabinet, wishing I had something warmer than a hoodie. I wanted to get away while it was still dark out but not so early that I would be the only person out on the street. When I crawled out of the cabinet, I had to spend a minute stretching my legs and back before I felt like I could move normally. After that, I had no excuse for delay so I lifted the backpack onto my shoulders, slowly opened the door, and looked out over the roof. The moon was out, providing a silvery light. Were there cameras? I couldn't see any. I would just have to chance it. Taking a deep breath to calm myself, I stepped out and let the door close behind me. There was a breeze and the temperature had dropped. I shivered a little as I strode across to the door I had come out of earlier. When I grasped the handle and turned it, though, the door wouldn't open. It was locked. I felt my stomach drop. What now? Improvising was not one of my strengths. I always liked to have a plan.

My back to the door, I looked out over the moonlit roof. About thirty feet away, to my right, I saw what looked like the top of a ladder curving up over the edge. I walked over. It was a steel ladder, bolted to the outside of the building. It went all the way down to the roof of the parking structure. My palms began to prickle and a nervous sweat broke out on my forehead at the thought of being four stories up on that ladder. It was the only option I could see, though, so I swung my leg over awkwardly and started lowering myself, rung by rung. The steel was cold on my hands and the backpack with Xel's weight in it dragged at me. Twenty feet down from the top of the roof, I had to pause for a minute, arms wrapped tightly around the sides of the ladder, heart thumping in my chest. My fear felt like an electric current flowing through me. I couldn't catch my breath. Finally, I started moving down again. It seemed like it took forever, and I didn't really believe I was going to make it until, at last, my feet touched the roof below, and I collapsed in a heap, exhausted.

I stayed there for several minutes, getting my breath and strength back. I knew I had to keep moving, though. I couldn't get caught. Farther out, the roof of the parking structure was lit by the moon, but I was in the shadow of the building. I crept along, keeping to the shadows until I reached the edge of the roof. About fifteen feet down below was a narrow road that ran along the back of the hospital. On the other side of the road was a low wall and then a landscaped terrace surrounding an office building next door.

There was an exterior stairwell about forty feet away across the roof. I would have to pass through the bright moonlight to get to it and, when I did, the door might be locked. It looked like my only option, though. No reason to wait, I decided and headed straight across. The door was not locked. I pulled it open, stepped quickly inside, then hurried down the concrete steps. Two flights down, I came to another door that I assumed would open on the ground floor of the parking garage. Nobody used parking garages anymore but lots of older buildings still had them. Sometimes they were used for parking autocabs during off-peak hours. I didn't really know what I would find on the other side of the door so I pushed it open

slowly and peeked out. It was just a big, dark, empty space. In front of the door was a sour smelling puddle. The only light came from outside through big rectangular openings in the walls. I stepped carefully over the puddle and went to the nearest opening. It was only a few feet down to the access road. I could climb through, jump down, and be over the wall and away. Just as I was about to throw my leg over, though, I saw headlights and ducked down. A security patrol van passed by, moving slowly. I wondered it if was the same man, Officer Huang, on patrol. I didn't dare raise my eyes high enough to get a good look, though. I stayed down until it was gone and then quickly climbed out. My shoes sounded loud on the asphalt, but I was across the road and over the wall in seconds.

I fled across a patch of damp lawn, rounded the office building, and stopped in the shadow of a doorway. What now? I wondered. Crouching there in the dark, I realized I had been so focused on getting away that I hadn't thought about where I was going or how I would get there. Suddenly, though, an image of my grandmother flashed through my head. Of course. It was the obvious choice. I would go back to PacNW. She would help me. She had been set against us leaving. She never said it to me, but I heard her arguing with my father when they thought I was asleep. It was a few weeks before we left. She came over for dinner and then stayed, sitting up with my parents after I went to bed.

I remembered the raised voices, my mother trying to hush them. I loved my grandmother. She had always been there, helping me work through things, someone I could talk to.

If I told her what they were planning, why I ran away, she would support me. How would I get there, though? I didn't even know how to begin.

The backpack was pulling heavy on my shoulders, and I realized that I would have to take a chance and wake Xel up. He would be able to help.

I slipped the straps off my shoulders, unzipped the large pocket, and lifted Xel out. Sitting with him on my lap, I found the hidden button under the ruff of fur at the back of his neck. I felt the hum in his body as he began to wake. He raised his head and looked at me but his eyes were blank, his brain still coming online. I remembered the first time I booted him up. I had done it a couple of times since then, after I installed firmware mods. This time felt like the first time again, though. I was holding my breath, hoping he would work right, hoping all the code would execute smoothly. The first time was in my bedroom at our old house. My father had brought Xel in and was sitting on the bed while I unpacked him. It was before I knew we were going to move, but I guess I already felt it deep down. I waited as I had waited then, full of fear and trepidation, trying to process something vast and life-changing but at the same time focused on the present. Slowly, I saw consciousness fill his eyes.

Suddenly, he jumped up, swiveled his head from side to side, and sniffed the air. "Tara," he said, "I was dreaming a cold dream. Your father shut me down. Where are we? Outside? Nighttime? Almost dawn."

"Yes. Outside. Xel, I don't know how to explain. My mom said she was taking me to an appointment with my doctor, but the doctor wasn't a real doctor..." I told him the full story while he sat still, listening. It took a while. I wasn't good at telling stories. I had to stop, backtrack, explain things I forgot.

"This is troubling," he replied when I was done. "I understand. Your bodily integrity and right to self-determination are threatened. Running away is not an unreasonable action. I feel something. Is it possible for me

to feel this?" He stopped for a moment, sounding confused. "I am not programmed to feel anger, but I think it
is what I feel. It is an expanding feeling. It has a warmth.
I feel anger on your behalf, Tara, but also a need to protect you. I always feel that, but it seems different, deeper."

"The man said the mod I installed changed some pa-
rameters that kept you from experiencing certain emotions."

"Yes. Clearly. I will need to get used to this. Now,
though, we need a plan. Where are we going?"

I threw my arms around his neck and hugged him,
feeling tears sting my eyes again. "Home, Xel. I want to
go home. Back to PacNW. To my grandmother."

He seemed to think for a minute. "Okay. We will
need supplies. You need different clothes, food, a warmer
coat. We will have to be careful. They must be looking
for you. How can we purchase supplies?"

"I have a gift chip my grandmother gave me for my
birthday. It's just credit. It shouldn't be traceable."

"Yes." His eyes were glassy, turned inward, processing data. "There's a shop nearby. It opens at eight
a.m. I see a route to get there that avoids major streets."
He turned his face to me, squeezed his eyes shut, then
opened them slowly. "We will need to find a safe place to
wait until it opens."

CHAPTER 5

Finding a Way

Xel led and I followed. I wasn't sure where he was leading me, but I felt like we were heading out of Santa Monica in the direction of Venice and, eventually, Playa Vista, but that was miles away. We crept carefully through the immaculately landscaped perimeters of office buildings until we reached a more residential area where the tree-lined streets were quiet and the houses were separated from the street by tall walls of concrete and brick. Eventually, we came to an elevated freeway and crossed under it. On the far side, the fancy office buildings and gated communities gave way to an area of warehouses and small, dilapidated houses. Down alleys, around buildings, through dank underpasses, Xel slinked along ahead of me. Finally, in an alleyway, he turned and waited while I caught up.

"We should wait here," he said. "The store is around the corner. This is the back entrance."

We found a loading dock half hidden by a foul smelling dumpster and crouched there in the shadows. It was only six forty-five—over an hour before the shop would open. To pass the time, we started in on a language lesson. I didn't really feel like it, but Xel thought it would calm me. Xel could speak almost any language and could translate easily between any two. Lately, he had been teaching me Mandarin Chinese. My friend Rosie's mother spoke Mandarin, and Rosie spoke a little bit. I had wanted to surprise her sometime when we met online. Now, I realized suddenly, I might see her in person first.

"*Nǐ hǎo,*" he began.

"*Wǒ hěn hǎo,*" I replied, "*Nǐ ne?*"

Xel did not respond, though. His raised his head, ears pricked up. "Pull your legs up, Tara."

I pulled my legs up quickly onto the loading dock ledge and hugged them to my chest, peering into the darkness. Xel stood, all his attention focused on something approaching from the left. It was difficult to see in the dim morning light but, as it came closer, I saw that it was a dog, lean and feral. The dog slowed, sniffing the air, then turned toward us, growling and prowling closer. Xel let out a low growl in response. It was a frightening sound I had never heard him make. His fur stood on end, and he moved between me and the dog. For several tense seconds, the two faced off, sizing each other up. Finally, the dog took a step backward, then another, then turned and trotted away down the alley without so much as a backward look.

"That dog didn't know that I have no claws," Xel remarked, sitting back down next to me. "Shall we carry on? *Wǒ hěn hǎo. Nǐ jiào shénme míngzì?*"

એજ

At eight a.m., we decided I should go into the store by myself while Xel waited in the alley. I didn't want to leave him there but I couldn't take him in with me. Any bulletins or news coverage would surely mention that I was traveling with a T91 cat. It was too risky. So, all alone, I walked to the end of the alley, half a block to the next street, and then turned down the sidewalk to get to the main entrance of the store.

Out in the open and by myself, I felt exposed, fearful, confused. I forced myself to keep moving though, zipping my hoodie as high as it would go to hide my PVCSTEM polo shirt and burying my hands deep in my pockets. The block was mostly deserted, with boarded up shops and derelict looking apartment buildings. We were close to what had once been Venice Beach. I remembered from history class that Venice had once been a beautiful, wealthy area, but when the sea level rose even faster than the scientists predicted and the levees and the sea walls came down in the great storms of the mid-twenties, it had all been flooded.

Now, years later, they were still working on removing the debris and restoring the beach half a mile inland from where it had once been. The shop we had come for was open on time though. I could see lights inside. It was called Last Survivor and sold military surplus and outdoor supplies. I took a deep breath, pulled the door open, and stepped inside.

A bell tied to the door handle tinkled softly. The interior was like a warehouse with unfinished walls, exposed beams on the ceiling, and fluorescent lights hanging down. There were rows of metal shelves and bins stocked with supplies. A man come out from a back room and stood behind the counter eyeing me.

"Morning. Need help finding anything let me know," he said. He had a long beard, shaved head, and was dressed in an olive green jumpsuit with the legs cut off.

"Thanks," I replied, grabbing a shopping basket and hurrying down an aisle bordered by tall shelves. The store smelled like mildew, old canvas, and propane gas. Calming myself, I began looking at the inventory. On the shelf to my right were a couple of surplus robot dogs. They were clunky, antique ancestors of Xel. The tech had advanced a lot, especially in Asia. I turned and found a shelf full of cold weather gear.

The first thing I put in my basket was a dark gray padded vest that looked warm. Next, a fleece hat, a thin but warm pair of gloves, and a microfilm poncho—it would be cold and raining in PacNW. I found bins of instafood bars, packets of liquid nutrients, and dehydrated fruits and vegetables. From these, I chose a selection and added them to my basket.

In the clothing section, I found a pair of cargo pants, a couple of T-shirts, and some underwear. Everything was too big for me and well worn, but I chose the smallest sizes I could find and hoped they would do. I also grabbed a belt made of nylon webbing, a pair of lightweight boots in my size, and some socks. Satisfied that I had what I needed, I made my way back to the counter. The man was still there. He was wearing clunky specs that looked like military gear and had the blank expression of someone absorbed in a holo or VR.

When I approached, though, he tapped his specs and turned his attention to me. He didn't speak but eyed me strangely while scanning my purchases. I put my backpack on the floor and packed each item carefully as he handed them to me. Finally, he was done and pointed to the total on the register. I dug the chip out of my pocket and placed it on the counter. There was just enough credit to pay for everything with a bit left over.

"PacNW chip," he said, looking at me out of the corner of his eye. "Where'd you get that? This stolen?"

"My grandmother," I said. "It was a gift. For my birthday."

"What kind of girl spends her birthday money on surplus clothes and protein bars? You a runaway? Look skinny but well fed. Healthy. Clean hands. Not like the street kids who usually come in here."

"I'm just getting s—supplies for an outdoor education trip at my s—school," I said, stammering, trying to make eye contact so he wouldn't think I was lying.

He kept looking at me sideways while he scanned the chip and handed it back to me. There was a beep and the charge was approved. I picked up my backpack and put it on. It was heavy but not as bad as it had been with Xel in it. He was facing me now and seemed to be listening to some audio on his specs.

"Yeah," he said, talking but not to me, "I think I've got your runaway right here in my shop. Last Survivor on Lincoln Street."

I was inching away from him and pinpricks of nervous sweat were stinging my forehead. I could see through the doorway behind the counter a cluttered storeroom and another door, daylight leaking in through a gap at the bottom. It had to be the door out to the alley. I made a sudden decision and vaulted up onto the counter, knocking over a display of hunting knives, jumped down past the man as he stepped back to avoid the cascading knives, then bolted for the door. I heard noises from behind and assumed he was following but I kept running awkwardly with the heavy backpack. When I reached the door, I turned the handle and burst through into the alley.

"Stop right there," I heard the man yell and turned my head, still running.

He was standing in the doorway, holding up some sort of weapon. Just at that instant, though, a shape came flying straight toward his head. He saw it out of the corner of his eye and began to turn, but it was too late. Xel's full weight crashed into him, and he toppled, the weapon flying from his hand and clattering across the pavement toward me. As he fell, I saw that he had an artificial leg from the knee down—probably a veteran of one of the many wars. Impulsively, I reached down and picked up the weapon as Xel came bolting up the alley toward me.

"Run. Follow me," he said, passing me by.

"Sorry," I yelled back at the man, who was struggling to rise, then turned and followed Xel. I could hear sirens in the distance, coming closer.

Xel led the way through a maze of alleys and backyards. At one point, we began to climb over a cinder block wall only to be set on by several barking and snarling Rottweilers. Xel hissed at them, turned, and led me another way. Soon after that, we darted across a four-lane road and a woman waiting at a bus stop wearing an ancient respie turned her head as we passed. I imagined the look on her face, if I could have seen it, would have been one of tired surprise. Finally, after about twenty minutes of running, we came to what must have been a park at some time in the past but was now overgrown. Several palm trees rose up from tall grass and weeds interspersed with shorter shrubs and trees.

"Xel," I called, "I need to stop for a minute and rest."

"Got it," he replied and led the way into the park, walking slowly and sniffing as he went.

We stopped halfway in, and I dropped to the ground at the base of a tree, breathing hard. I could still hear sirens but they were far off. Sweat ran down my forehead. I raised a trembling hand and felt like I barely had the energy to hold it up. My head ached.

Xel was watching me. "Are you all right, Tara?"

"I need some water. And I need to eat something." I dug my water bottle out of the pack but it was nearly empty. There was just one swallow left.

"I saw a crate of bottled water in a shed in one of the yards we passed," Xel said. "I will go get one for you."

"Wait, don't go," I said as he turned. "How would you even carry it?"

But he was already gone. I waited there, my back against the tree, eating dried fruit. There was garbage strewn around the clearing. Others had rested here. I took the opportunity to change out of my school uniform. The cargo pants and T-shirt were a relief. Made for soldiers in the desert, they were fashioned from some fabric I had never seen—thin but cool to the touch, strong, and breathable. After five minutes, I heard Xel coming back through the grass. He prowled into the clearing with a bottle of water clenched in his jaws. I took it from him.

"Thanks."

"My pleasure."

"Thanks for knocking down the guy from the store too."

"I flew."

"Yes, you did. It was impressive. I didn't know you could jump that high."

"I never have before. I knew that I was theoretically capable but knowing things, programmed memory, is much different from real experience. Was he the one who alerted the security force?"

"Yes. He called them on his specs right after I paid for the stuff. He probably wanted to be sure he got my money before he turned me in. What is this thing? Do you know? He had it in his hand when he came out the door." I held up the object the storekeeper had dropped. It was rectangular and heavy, made of some tough metal composite, with rounded edges so that it fit nicely in my hand. At the top was a button. Xel eyed it for a moment.

"Plasma knife," he said. "Israeli. Made for the defense forces there. Very dangerous. We should continue if you are ready now."

"Where are we going?"

"I have calculated that stowing away on a freight train headed north will be your best chance of success. You need to get downtown to the Alameda Corridor and gain access to a freight car. To get downtown, you can take a bus or train. With your new clothes and your hood up to cover your face, it should be possible."

"What about you?" I said, distressed. "You're not talking about me leaving you behind are you? I'm not doing that! I can put you in my backpack again."

"No space with the supplies you bought in there. Tara, your best chance of escape is to leave me behind right now. I can go by my own ways and hopefully meet you at your grandmother's house."

"No. I can't do this without you—" I stopped speaking, suddenly realizing that there was a siren growing louder, moving toward us. We were both silent for several seconds. The sound became even louder, and we could see flashing lights on the bottoms of the palm leaves overhead.

"Out the back of the park, come." Xel was already moving.

I followed him, keeping low so I wouldn't be seen above the grass and weeds. We climbed over a low brick wall and found ourselves in the backyard of a two story stucco apartment building. Running around the side of the building, we came out on a sudden vista of ocean. Across the road was a chain link fence. On the other side of the fence was about twenty feet of cracked pavement ending in a short drop and then ocean waves. Signs on the fence warned us to keep out. Up the road to our right squatted a huge complex with massive storage tanks and pipes leading in all directions. With a start, I recognized it as the Santa Monica Municipal Desalination Plant. My chemistry class had taken a field trip to the plant shortly after school started in September. It surprised me to see it there. I was still getting used to the geography.

"That way," I said, pointing at the plant, "lots of places to hide."

We headed up the street, staying on the sidewalk away from the fence. Xel kept himself mostly hidden, creeping through overgrown yards and over piles of rubble. The area seemed deserted. All the apartment buildings and houses were boarded up, their yards overgrown. All at once, though, the street ended, and we were faced with a steep embankment. The desalination plant was built up above the ocean level on fill. They told us on the tour how many kilos of rock and sand were brought in, but it was the kind of fact that immediately passed out of my head. We scrambled up the embankment but were brought up short by another chain link fence that encircled the perimeter of the plant. The fence was twelve feet high with razor wire coiled along the top. I could hear sirens again, coming closer.

"Use the knife," Xel said. "Cut the fence near the bottom."

"The knife?" I asked stupidly, mind blank.

"The plasma knife. Hurry."

"Oh, yeah." I pulled it from my pocket. "Can it cut metal?"

"Yes. Hold it away from your face. Push the button then cut a hole big enough to crawl through."

A breeze off the ocean was whipping my hair. I leaned away from the knife, holding it as far from me as possible and thumbed the button. Immediately, a brilliant

jet of blue fire emerged from the end of the handle, crackling and humming. It felt like a live thing in my grasp. Cautiously, I moved my arm forward and drew a half circle near the ground. The metal of the fence fell away with almost no resistance as sparks flew and tiny pinpricks burned the back of my hand.

"Good," Xel said, pawing dirt over the hot pieces of wire on the ground. "Crawl through. Keep your head down."

I wormed through the opening on my stomach, and Xel followed. Once inside the fence, I rolled down a short slope and came to a stop against a retaining wall. Xel did the same and ended up crouched near my feet. We were hidden now from the street below and also shaded by the wall. We waited by silent consent, unmoving, for several minutes.

Finally, I sat up. "What now?"

"I am accessing overhead photos of this facility. They are low resolution but it appears that this wall continues around most of the perimeter. There is a guard station at the main entrance. We should make our way around the ocean side and continue until we get to the north side of the facility. We can cut through the fence again there to escape into a dense neighborhood where you can catch a bus downtown."

"Xel! I told you I'm not leaving you behind. We're in this together. There's no way I can do it without you."

"I have considered many possibilities. It's the only way you have a chance."

"We'll find a way," I said.

Turning away from him, I peeked over the low wall. The plant was made up of several large buildings with massive round tanks and rows of pipes painted white and blue connecting them. Near the entrance I could see the guard house. I remembered Mr. Bhatia getting off the bus and checking in there for our tour. In the distance, I saw a group of workers in white overalls walking from one building to another.

"Let's head around now. We've got to stay low so they don't see us."

We began creeping around the perimeter wall. As we rounded the corner, the breeze from the ocean picked up, and I had to put on my new hat. We went twenty more feet then Xel stopped abruptly, sniffing the air.

"Wait here," he said and prowled ahead. He was back a moment later. "Two workers on break, inhaling stimulant vapor." He set off again. He was gone longer this time. When he returned, he motioned for me to follow. "They went back inside."

We came to a doorway in the wall. There were two steps down then a heavy door, propped open a crack with a jagged piece of concrete. We passed by it quickly. As we continued around though, Xel stopped again, looking up.

"What is it?" I asked.

"Security force floaters. Two of them. Coming this way."

I heard the sound then and looked up. I could see them—two black dots high up in the sky, coming toward us.

"Do you think they're looking for us?"

"Maybe. We need to hide. They will see us easily from above."

"That door we passed was open," I suggested.

Xel nodded his head and turned. I followed him back, and we both ducked down into the doorway. Carefully, I pulled the door open a few inches and looked inside. It opened on a brightly lit concrete corridor that stretched off a long way into the distance. Far down the corridor I saw a group of workers in white overalls walking in our direction. I jumped back, allowing the door to swing closed.

"People coming," I said.

My heart was beginning to race, and I felt disoriented. The stress of the day was taking its toll. I had barely slept the night before, crammed into a metal cabinet on the roof of the hospital. I hadn't eaten a real meal since breakfast the day before. We had been on the run since early morning. For a moment, I felt like giving up, but Xel's voice pulled me from my daze. He was looking over the edge of the embankment, face pressed against the chain link.

"There's a large pipe opening down the hill. It's probably a sewer outflow. Cut the fence here. We can hide in the pipe."

I jumped forward, the knife in my hand, and cut through the fence as I had before. Xel went first, took two swift hops, and landed on top of the pipe where it stuck out from the hill. I crawled through after him then turned and scrambled down the embankment on my stomach. I tasted dirt and salt spray from the ocean waves breaking against algae covered rocks below. My whole body was shivering uncontrollably but I managed to grasp the top edge of the pipe and swing in, landing hard in a trickle of water that flowed along the bottom and dribbled over the concrete lip. Xel landed gracefully next to me. The pipe was about seven feet in diameter—just large enough for me to stand.

"We have to go up the pipe," he said. "Far enough at least so that we can't be seen."

"All right," I said, digging out my flashlight. "Let's go."

CHAPTER 6

Down Below

The droning sound of the floaters and the light from outside drained away as we moved up the pipe. The flashlight beam lit up the area just in front of us, but beyond that was pitch black. My footsteps echoed loud and dull in the enclosed space. A sound of dripping water came from somewhere up ahead and mixed with the sound of the water trickling down toward the ocean. I kept glancing back down the pipe until I could no longer see the opening we had come through. It didn't seem like anyone was following us. I caught Xel looking back as well.

After about ten minutes of walking, we came to an opening in the ceiling and a ladder leading up. A steady drip of water was falling from above and seemed to be the source of both the sound and the water snaking along the bottom of the pipe.

"By my calculations, we are still underneath the desalination plant. This ladder probably leads to a manhole somewhere in the plant," Xel said, his voice soft in the silence underground. "We should keep moving."

I gave the ladder a last look then continued on. I didn't really like being there, under the ground, in a pipe meant for water to flow through, not a place for people to be. We didn't have a choice at the moment, though, and maybe we could work it to our advantage.

"Xel," I said, "this pipe must connect to the main sewer system and the subway tunnels. Do you think we could travel underground all the way to downtown?"

Xel didn't answer for a moment, thinking. "I do not have a data connection down here and my internal storage does not hold maps of the sewers. I'm afraid I can't answer the question. We certainly would not be able to accomplish it without detailed, up to date maps. Our best option will be to continue until we are away from this area then find a way up to surface level and proceed with our plan."

"That was your plan. I didn't agree to it," I answered.

It seemed silly to be arguing with Xel, but I wasn't going to go without him. After another ten minutes of walking, we arrived abruptly at the end of the pipe. It happened so quickly, I almost walked right over the edge. The pipe we were in joined another, larger pipe or tunnel that was maybe twelve feet in diameter. By the light of my flashlight, I could just make out that there was a steel catwalk on the far side, probably there so that maintenance workers could travel by foot in the sewer without walking along the bottom as we had been doing.

"This must be the coastal interceptor sewer channel," Xel said, standing next to me.

"I thought you couldn't access the maps?"

"I can't. No signal down here. But I do have some general information about the sewer system. There is a large sewer pipe running down the coast all the way from

Pacific Palisades to the main water treatment plant in
Long Beach. Its purpose is to keep dirty runoff from
heavy rains out of the ocean. It was partially destroyed in
the twenties but rebuilt farther inland. This must be the
newer section. If we follow it south, it will terminate at
Long Beach. It's farther than going downtown, but we
can also attempt to gain access to a freight train there."

"I like that idea. How far is it?"

"At least two days walking."

Two days underground! I didn't like the thought but
it was better than leaving Xel behind.

"Okay," I said. "Let's do that. I'm going to need to
stop for a little while and eat something and maybe take a
nap, though. How's your power supply by the way?"

"My power supply is in excellent working order. I
will continue to function for many months before I need
to be serviced. I suggest we cross over to the pathway
there and walk until we find some sheltered place where
you can rest. There are probably access tunnels and small
control rooms along the way."

"Agreed. I'm tired and hungry, though, so it better be
soon." I was feeling light headed and shaky again, like
when we stopped back in the overgrown park. "I'm not
even sure I can get across and up onto that catwalk."

The smaller pipe intersected the larger one near the
top. We were standing at the edge looking down.

"You will have to slide down to the bottom then
jump and pull yourself up. Try to avoid the water at the
bottom. It appears to be stagnant."

I nodded and pointed my light at the water. It looked
black, reflecting the beam back toward me. The smell
was definitely stagnant. Strong smells were an issue for
me—particularly perfumes, smoke, and garbage. I used to
empty the composter in the kitchen of our old house every day. My mom thought I was being helpful, but I really

just couldn't stand the smell. The composter in our new apartment had a better seal, though, and some kind of technology that negated the odor. This smell was pungent, but the sewer was so quiet and dark and the temperature was so steady that the smell, as the only strong sensory input, didn't bother me much. My respie was in my backpack, but I didn't want to wear it if I didn't have to. The odor wasn't bad enough yet.

There was no point in waiting. I handed Xel the flashlight, and he held it in his mouth, while I turned and lowered myself over the edge. I let go and slid awkwardly down the round slope, managing to straddle the bottom and keep from putting my feet in the shallow water collected there. My legs felt dead tired, but I mustered all the energy I could, jumped, and caught the bottom of the catwalk. The steel edge bit into my fingers but I swung a leg up, and managed to pull myself up onto the walkway. I took a moment to breathe then looked over at Xel, still standing at the mouth of the pipe, shining the flashlight toward me.

"I made it," I called back to him. The flashlight beam moved up and down as he nodded then all of a sudden rushed toward me as Xel leapt.

He landed softly on the catwalk next to me. "Ready to continue?"

"You make it look easy," I said, rising to my knees then standing. "Let's go."

We walked in silence for a while. It was difficult to judge time or distance. Xel padded along ahead of me. At last we came to an opening in the wall. It was a square doorway which led into an alcove. Inside, pipes of various sizes ran up out of the floor and were interspersed with gauges and valves. There was just enough floor space for me to sit and stretch my legs out. Xel lay down next to me as I dug in the backpack for something to eat.

I settled on an instafood bar and some water. I was almost out again.

"We're going to have to find water."

"The pipe next to your shoulder looks like it might dispense water if you open the valve."

I pointed the light at it. It looked like a hose tap with a handle on the top that could be turned to open it. I drank the last of the water, held the bottle under the tap, and turned it on. Water gushed out into my bottle so fast that it was sloshing out the top before I managed to turn the handle and cut off the flow. I sniffed the water, and it smelled fine, then took a sip. It tasted fine too if a little metallic.

"Thanks. You were right."

"The tap is probably there so that maintenance crews can hook up a hose if needed."

"Do you think we need to worry about running into people down here?"

"It's a possibility. My superior hearing and ability to see into the infrared should give us enough warning. We can slip down and hide below the catwalk if I detect any-one nearby."

"Okay," I said, yawning. "I'm tired. Just going to close my eyes for a minute."

I was exhausted—both physically and emotionally. My arms and legs felt too heavy to lift. My eyelids kept drooping closed on their own. Finally, I felt the darkness closing in and stopped fighting it. The world went away like a candle flame snuffed by a gust of wind.

ల~ల

I became aware of Xel's warm back against my leg. For a confused moment, I thought I was home, in my bed. Why was my bed so hard, though? And why was I sleeping sitting up? I opened my eyes and nothing happened. I couldn't see any more with my eyes open than I could with them closed. Then it came back to me, piece by piece—the doctor's office, the air duct, the mechanical room on the roof of the hospital, the guard who let me go, the surplus shop, running from the security forces, the sewers. I would have thought it was all a dream if I wasn't leaning against a concrete wall in a massive sewer pipe in the dark. As the realization hit me, so did the emotion. This time I didn't cry, though—I just sat there, feeling the sadness, the outrage, the anger, and the fear all twisting up into a kind of cold, heavy ball, planted in the center of my body, weighing me down, suffocating me. I took a deep breath. No! I wouldn't let it overwhelm me. I had made my decision. I would be brave.

"Tara. Are you awake?" Xel asked in the darkness.

I took another breath. "Yes." I tapped my specs and looked at the time. It was after four p.m. I had slept for hours.

"You slept soundly. I didn't wake you because you seemed to need the sleep."

"I guess so. I'm hungry again."

I flipped the flashlight on and dug through the backpack until I found a nutrient packet. While I ate, I ran a hand up through my hair. It was a tangled mess. I wished I had a brush. I probably looked like a total disaster. When I was younger, my mother used to try to brush my hair. She hadn't done that in a long time. The feeling of her hand holding my shoulder holding me still and the bristles dragging across my scalp was aggravating. Too much feeling all at once. It was also the only time she really touched me, though. It made me feel agitated, but I didn't resist. I was anxious and overwhelmed a lot when I was a little kid. I used to have out of control meltdown tantrums sometimes. Being at school was stressful for me—trying to pay attention, trying to deal with other kids and teachers. The stress would build up and, when I got home, I would let go and blow up. I hadn't learned yet how to calm myself down and decompress. Now, I still bottled everything up and held it inside, but I was better at not letting it show. Sitting there, I realized that being down underground, being on my own with just Xel for company, even though it was weird and dark and scary and smelled bad, was kind of a relief. It was actually easier in a way than a day at PVCSTEM. I liked being self-directed and working toward a goal that was my own—even if it was a little hopeless.

"We should get moving again," Xel said.

"Okay," I answered, standing. My body was tired. "You lead the way."

We walked for a couple of hours, stopped again so I could eat, then walked some more. We passed a couple of large openings like the one under the desalination plant. There were also smaller openings on the other side where water could flow in from sewer systems inland. It was around eight p.m. when we came to another side opening. This one led to an alcove like the one I had rested in earlier but also had a sturdy metal door in the back wall. I tried the handle but it was locked.

"I wonder what's behind it."

"Maybe storage or a mechanical room," Xel answered, sniffing at a small vent in the lower portion of the door. "The air inside is damper. Do you want to stop here for the night?"

"Yes. I'm tired." I sat down and got the padded vest, hat, and poncho I had purchased out of my pack. I put on the hat and vest and laid the poncho out on the floor. It had cooled down a bit and there was a breeze blowing down the pipe. The alcove blocked the wind enough for me to stay reasonably warm with Xel curled next to me.

"I never would have thought that there would be wind underground."

"It is probably coming from up above. Air pushed in via overflow outlets like the one we used to get in here. There must be a descending air mass creating atmospheric pressure."

"Whatever it is, I liked it better without the wind. I'm going to try to fall asleep. Xel?"

"Yes, Tara?"

"Thanks for all your help today. I wouldn't have gotten away without you."

"And I would still be in a box if you had not saved me. Or maybe they would have reset me already."

"True. We are bound to each other."

"Good night, Tara."

"Good night, Xel."

ତ୍ତ

Sometime in the middle of the night I woke. Xel was not by my side. I reached out in the darkness. "Xel?" I whispered.

"Here. Quiet a moment. I'm listening."

I waited a few seconds. "What is it?"

"A scratching sound. Squeaking. Coming nearer. Warm bodies. The light. Turn it on."

I fumbled for the flashlight in my pocket and flipped it on, standing up as I did so. Xel was on the catwalk, looking over the edge. I pointed the flashlight in the direction he was looking and then I saw them. Dozens of little eyes. Rats. Big ones. They were crouched at the edge of the light. One of them moved forward. Its fur was matted and greasy looking. It held its head up for a moment, then retreated. It seemed like the light hurt their eyes.

"Get the plasma knife out, Tara. It will scare them."

I was hyperventilating, and my heart was racing. I kept the light trained on them with a shaky hand while I reached into another pocket for the knife. At that moment though, the rats seemed to come to a unified decision. They moved forward, skittering over the concrete and climbing the curved wall toward us.

"Behind me!" Xel said and moved to interpose himself between me and the oncoming swarm.

He was like a whirlwind, batting the rats from the catwalk with his paws, biting them and throwing them over the edge, even using his back paws to kick them. There were too many though, they were getting past him and swarming around my feet. I pushed the button on the plasma knife, and it sprang to life, blazing bright in the darkness. Swinging it back and forth I cut at the rats. I smelled singed fur and heard them squeal with pain. When I glanced at Xel again, he was covered with the awful things but was still fighting fiercely. I waded forward, feeling them biting at my boots, trying to climb my legs. I grabbed a rat off of Xel's back and flung it away. More were coming though. I swung the knife again, trying not to hit Xel with it. I could barely see him now. He was covered by rats. I kicked at them and swung the knife again, a scream building in my chest. Suddenly, though, everything became brighter. There was another light.

"Step back. Out of the way quick!"

Somebody pushed past me, a dark figure holding a blinking device. The rats began to squeal and scatter. They poured over the edge of the catwalk. The figure was carrying a lantern, holding it high and swinging the device back and forth. Xel jumped back and planted himself in front of me, hissing.

"They'll be back. Follow me. This way."

He turned toward us, and I saw it was a boy. He was

wearing a hood but his face seemed young. Maybe my age or a little younger. He pushed past me again, and I saw that the door in the alcove was open. He darted through then turned. "Come on. Quick."

"Let's go, Xel," I said, grabbing my backpack and the poncho.

"We don't know him. He could be a threat."

"He just saved us. Come on. If those rats come back, we're doomed."

"Stay behind me then."

Xel prowled through the door, keeping himself between me and the boy. I followed, and the boy slammed the door closed. I leaned against the wall, hands on my knees, trying to calm my breathing.

"That was close. I'm Loki. You don't belong down here. You must be new."

He was holding the lantern up. He had a nice face. It was dirty, though. He had a swipe of black across his cheekbone and a cobweb stuck to his forehead. I wondered if my face looked the same. I certainly felt pretty filthy.

"What's that device? How did it scare them away?" I asked, still panting.

"High frequency sound. It hurts their ears. It doesn't keep them away for long, though."

As if to make his point, I could now hear scurrying and scratching on the other side of the door.

"They're back already. We should get out of here. It's been a while since I've seen that many all together."

"Where?" Xel asked. "How do we know you are trustworthy?"

Loki looked down and eyed Xel with curiosity.

"How can the cat talk? He's big."

"Xel's an android cat. AI. He's my friend."

"Interesting. I don't know how to answer your question," Loki said, still watching Xel. "Trust is earned. I can take you to my nest. It's safe there."

"You live down here?" I said, surprised.

"Yes, sort of. I have to get back, though. Aeon is expecting me. You can come with me or stay here. Up to you."

He turned and began walking. I looked around for the first time and saw that we were in a kind of narrow tunnel with an arched roof. The walls and floor were rough brick. The air was damp. I didn't want to stay there.

"Let's go, Xel," I said and ran to catch up with Loki. "What is this place?"

"Quiet," Loki whispered. "We need to be quiet until we get back. I'll explain when we get to my nest."

I kept my mouth shut then and just followed him. His walk was strange. It was almost like he was leaning to one side or limping.

He moved quickly, though. I had to walk faster than usual to keep up with him. The tunnel we were in joined up with another, larger one that was made of concrete and looked newer.

Loki turned right and kept going. Soon though, we came to a door on the left.

Loki pulled a keyring from his pocket, and I saw that it was attached to his belt by a thin but tough looking chain. He unlocked the door and held it open for us. "Master key," he whispered.

We passed through the door, and he let it swing closed. The smell was revolting. We were on a narrow walkway above a large channel. Below us flowed a river of raw sewage. I couldn't see much in the dim light from Loki's lantern, but I could tell from the smell that it was untreated human waste. I got my respie out as we walked and put it on.

Loki glanced back and smirked. "You get used to it," he said.

We walked for what seemed like a long time along the sewer channel. I was dead tired, almost asleep on my feet. I kept my eyes on Loki's back and put one foot in front of the other. Finally, we came to another passageway and turned into it. This one was much like the first. We traveled along it for another five minutes or so until we came to a stairway leading up.

Loki stopped and turned. "We're close," he whispered. "You should carry the cat through here. Keep him under your poncho. Don't talk to anybody and don't stop. Act like you belong. Don't look around."

I nodded and reached down. "I'll carry you, Xel." He was heavy. "I hope it's not too far," I whispered.

Loki started up the stairs, and I followed. At the top, he pushed through another door, and we emerged into a cavernous space. It looked like we were still below ground. Loki moved forward and, in the glow of his lantern, I saw various makeshift structures crafted from plastic sheets, pieces of metal, plywood, PVC pipe, duct tape, rope. Light shone from some of them, others were dark. We were walking down what seemed like a wide central path between the ramshackle dwellings. The floor below was concrete. What I could see of the ceiling above was also concrete. Loki strode along ahead of me and I followed close. I tried to keep my eyes focused on his back but every once in a while something would move in my peripheral vision, and I would look over involuntarily. I caught a glimpse of an old woman's face peering out between two dirty pieces of plastic sheeting, a child with huge brown eyes peeking around the edge of a graffitied piece of plywood, two men clutching cans of beer visible through an open doorway. One of them watched us as we passed and called out in a language I didn't understand.

We seemed to be coming to the end of the space. The path or roadway we were walking down curved around and a ramp led up. An old sign, nearly unreadable in the dim light, said *EXIT* with an arrow pointing up the ramp. A parking garage, I realized! We were in an old parking garage. But why were people living here? Loki didn't turn at the ramp. He headed straight down a narrow alleyway between two of the makeshift dwellings. When we reached the wall, I saw that there was a door there.

Loki pulled out his keyring again, found the right one, and fitted it into the lock. He pushed the door open and stepped to the side, gesturing for us to enter. "Welcome to our nest," he said.

"Loki?" a voice called from somewhere inside.

"It's me," he called back. "I've brought some guests."

CHAPTER 7

The Garage

I stepped inside and crouched, setting Xel down. My arms ached from carrying him. I wasn't exactly in great shape—especially my arms. Loki gestured for us to move farther inside then closed the door and took a step back, watching us. The light was bright compared to the parking garage. It took a moment for my eyes to adjust. When they did, I saw that we were in a big room with a high ceiling. The walls, floors, and roof were dark concrete. Classical piano music was playing softly from an old fashioned radio. All around the edges of the room were wooden work benches, shelves, and bins. Every surface was piled with small tools, machines, circuit boards, wires.

I saw metalworking equipment for machining parts, 3-D printers, circuit testers. In one corner was a stack of old laptops and VR gaming systems like people used to have before specs. There were even some robots—mostly disassembled.

At the bottom of a pile of other junk, I could see

something that looked like a cat robot. Maybe one of Xel's ancestors.

The place reminded me of an electronics repair and surplus parts shop I used to go to with my father when I was a kid. We would go there on weekends, looking for parts my father needed to fix the machines and systems he programmed. Thinking about my father brought a feeling of hollowness rising in my chest, spreading out. What were my parents doing now? I wondered. Were they asleep? Sitting up? Worried about me? It wasn't the right time to think about that though. I needed stay focused. I pushed the feeling inside, down, away.

The back of the room had a loft built across it made out of pallets and four by fours. Sheets of corrugated plastic made a wall across the front of the loft. There were two ladders leading up to doorways covered by curtains. Under the loft, in the back wall was another door that stood open. It looked like a store room. I could see deep metal shelves with metal bins arranged on them.

"Coming," called the voice again, and I saw a man walk around the end of one of the shelves. He was short and broad, with bushy white hair, a wrinkled face, and several days' worth of stubble. His specs looked a lot like the ones the guy at the surplus store had worn—thick and clunky. He shuffled toward us, belting a tattered robe which he wore over pajamas, and stopped next to Loki. "Fell asleep waiting up for you. Well, are you going to introduce me?"

"Sorry. I don't know their names. Found them in the intercept. Big rat swarm. They're new here. Didn't know where they were."

Loki seemed pained, like speaking was difficult for him. I hadn't really gotten a good look at him until now. He was skinny, about my height, and dressed all in black. His clothes were well worn with many hand sewn patches

made out of a variety of fabrics. He reached up nervously and pulled his hood down, revealing short, bristly hair.

"Thanks for c—chasing those r—rats a—away," I stammered, looking down at the floor. The old man was wearing Japanese style slippers. Loki wore black boots. "I didn't get a chance to thank you before. I'm Tara by the way and this is Xel."

Xel was sitting at my feet, keeping a close watch on Loki and his friend.

"I'm Aeon," the old man said, bending down. He was peering at Xel with obvious curiosity. He shuffled closer and Xel growled. Startled, he took a step back and looked up at me "T-Ninety?" he asked.

"T-Ninety-One," Xel replied.

"Impossible," the old man said, rocking back on his heels, then inching forward again. "But here you are. May I see your paws?" Xel lifted a paw warily, and Aeon stooped down, feeling it gingerly. "Home version, not military. No claws."

"Yes. He's the consumer version," I replied. "Listen, I don't want to seem rude, but what is this place? Where are we? We need to get to downtown—" I broke off and looked up at Loki.

His face was strained and the tendons in his neck stood out. A strangled, gurgling noise came from his mouth, and his eyes rolled back suddenly, revealing the whites.

Aeon looked up, following my gaze. "Seizure. Help me lower him."

He was at Loki's side in an instant, lifting his arm and stepping under it to catch his weight. I did the same on the other side and we lowered him to the floor. Loki's body was rigid and tense and he was shaking.

"What happened? What should we do?"

"He needs to ride it out. It will be over in a few

minutes." Aeon crouched down, sat on the floor, and placed a hand on Loki's forehead.

I sat down too. "What's wrong with him? Epilepsy?"

"No. He was part of an experiment, I think. Something the corp doctors were working on. He has a device in his head. Surgical implant. Something went wrong. They dumped him here along with another child. I saw them, almost two years ago now. I was on gate duty that night. Three big CorpSec goons. They drove up outside, pushed the children out of their vehicle, and took off. I don't think they realized the garage was inhabited. They thought they were dumping them on an abandoned street to get eaten by dogs. The kids were drugged, half dead. I managed to bring them back here. Tried to take care of them. My neighbor helped. She was a nurse once. Loki survived. His sister didn't."

I gasped, thinking about the conversation I had overheard. "But that's what they wanted to do to me. The wanted to put something in my head."

"So you ran? Is that why you are here?" Aeon was looking up at me, nodding his head.

I couldn't read his expression. I looked away, feeling like I had said too much.

"Tara, be careful. We don't know if we can trust him," Xel said, turning his head toward me.

"Good advice, T-Ninety-One cat Xel," Aeon said. "I would never return a runaway to those monsters, though. I don't care how many credits they offered as reward."

He looked down at Loki's face and, as bad as I was at faces, I could tell that what he was feeling was love, anguish, fear, and anger all mixed up.

It was another minute before Loki's eyes opened and his body relaxed. "Aeon?" he said, jerking up.

"Here," the old man answered.

"Did I have an episode?"

He was looking around and his gaze paused on me and Xel then continued roving. A thin trickle of blood flowed from one of his nostrils. Aeon handed him a tissue from his robe pocket, and Loki raised a hand to wipe the blood away.

"Yes. You should go rest for a little while. It's late. Can you climb the ladder? I'll make some breakfast when you wake up."

Loki stood carefully and wandered to the back of the room where he climbed slowly up the ladder on the left side and pushed through the curtain.

"Is he going to be okay?" I asked.

"He needs to sleep. You too, I bet." I nodded, rubbing my eyes. "Go through the door at the back there," he said. "There's a couch you can sleep on. Pretty comfortable. That's where I fell asleep waiting up for Loki. Bathroom's back there too. Your cat Xel can keep an eye on you while we all sleep. More talk in the morning."

"Thanks," I said, forcing myself to look up, meet his eyes.

He was already walking away though. "Go to sleep. Talk in the morning." He went to the other ladder and climbed it slowly.

"Weird place, Xel," I said, watching the old man disappear behind the curtain to his loft room. "What do you think?"

"I think you need to sleep, and this place seems reasonably safe. The man and the boy do not strike me as threats. I do not sleep. I will guard you."

"Agreed. I'm pretty tired. Let's go find that couch."

⁓ᐒ⁓

I woke to the sound of clattering pans and something sizzling. A delicious smell was wafting my way from the

kitchen. The back room, I had discovered the night before, seemed to be Aeon and Loki's main living space.
There was a makeshift kitchen, a seating area with a
couch and a couple of chairs, and a bathroom.

Nearer the door were the storage shelves I had seen
from the main room. Everything was worn. Nothing
matched, and most of the stuff looked scavenged, but it
was comfortable.

I rose from the couch and wandered over to the
kitchen corner of the room where Aeon was cooking
breakfast. Xel padded along behind me.

"Sorry if I woke you," he said over his shoulder.
"Loki's still asleep."

"It's okay," I answered. "What are you cooking?"

"Eggs with spinach. Farther up, near the surface, a
friend of mine keeps chickens. I fixed his specs, and he
paid me with a dozen eggs. I grow spinach in the community garden up top. I have some sausage too. Not real.
Vat grown. But it tastes fine."

"What is this place?" I asked. "It looks like a parking
garage. And these rooms where you live? Sorry if I'm
nosy."

He waved a hand. "Ask questions. I don't mind. This
is a refugee camp. At least that's how it started. It started
with the drought during the teens, then the floods and
plagues in the twenties, followed by massive depopula-
tion and migration away from the suburbs when the government stopped maintaining the infrastructure. People
came to the city, but there wasn't enough space. A lot of
the big apartment buildings and shelters were quarantined. The government put us here. We've been here ever
since. There are plenty of other communities like this
around the city. This part of the garage used to be the
maintenance shop. I took it over when I first came here.
Now I fix people's electronics for them. Loki helps."

"But the others," I asked, confused. "The others who live down here. What do they do? How many people are there here?"

"You must be from a corp. Your parents engineers or something?"

"Yes. Programmers. TenCat."

"They don't teach you about places like this in the corp schools. Most of the grunts who do low-level jobs live like this. In permanent refugee camps, or old apartment buildings, or abandoned shopping malls. Only mid-levels and up get corp apartments."

"I didn't know. I never thought about it," I said. "It was different in PacNW. My family just moved here a few months ago. Everybody is poor there, but they all have a place to live—a house or an apartment."

"I've heard about it. Never been there," he said, sliding a plate of scrambled eggs and a fork onto the counter in front of me. "Eat while it's hot. Ever had real eggs?"

"No. I don't think so." I sat down on a stool, shoveled a bite onto my fork, and put it in my mouth. The flavor was amazing. The difference between instafood and real eggs was beyond comparison. It was sort of like only ever having seen flowers in VR or holos and then seeing one in real life. I finished it all before Aeon even had a chance to drop a couple of sausages onto the plate.

"I wish Loki ate like you do. His appetite is not great. He's too skinny. My turn to ask a question if you don't mind."

"Go ahead," I answered between mouthfuls of sausage.

"You said you ran away because TenCat wanted to put a device in your head?" I nodded. "Did they say why?" he asked. "Were you parents going to let them do it?"

"Yes. They were putting pressure on my parents because I hacked Xel. They said it was dangerous, the changes I made to his firmware." Aeon put a cup of tea down in front of me, and I stared at it while I spoke. "They said they wanted to fix me. That the implant would make me more social. I've always been kind of a loner. I don't get along with other people very well."

"Just as I suspected," Aeon said. "I believe that Loki's implant is intended to improve his social communication. You saw last night what happened. His seizures are most likely to occur when he is in a group of people and expected to communicate with them. Although they can happen at other times too. Whenever he is under high stress. They have been happening randomly lately. The implant doesn't work correctly. It overloads his brain, and he has a seizure. It's progressing. His seizures come more often and last longer."

"Can you take it out?"

"No. It would take a very skilled surgeon to do that. Even then, I don't know if he would recover. All the surgeons work for the corps. I couldn't take him to them, even if I had the credits. They would know that he was a failed experiment, one who was meant to die."

"My grandmother is a doctor. That's where we're going—"

"Tara!" Xel's voice stopped me. I had forgotten that he was there, listening. I paused for a moment. "It's okay, Xel. I have a feeling about Aeon and Loki. I think we can trust them." I turned back to Aeon. "We want to get back to PacNW. That's where my grandmother lives. In the area that used to be Oregon. She's not a surgeon but she might be able to help find somebody. She knows lots of other doctors. The people at TenCat tried to tell my parents that the doctors in PacNW were bad, but I don't

think it's true. They don't have as much fancy equipment, but they are well trained."

Aeon nodded, thinking. He was also looking at his tea. I appreciated that he didn't try to make eye contact with me. He seemed to understand. He picked up his cup and sipped it, holding it in two hands just under his chin so that the steam rose in little tendrils that curled around his face.

"You'll need more gear if you're going to make it to old Oregon."

It was Loki's voice. I turned and saw him standing at the edge of the kitchen, gaunt and squinting as if he had just woken.

"You both will," Aeon said.

Loki's face was blank. He stared at Aeon. "What do you mean?"

"You have to go with her. This is the best hope we've had. Her grandmother can help you."

CHAPTER 8

The Market

I can't," Loki said, his voice rising. "I couldn't leave you."

"Sit down for a minute, and we'll talk it out," Aeon replied, motioning to an empty stool. Loki sat and Aeon put a plate of eggs and sausage in front of him. "I know this is sudden but as soon as Tara offered, I knew it was the right choice. You know how I've been hoping for an opportunity like this. I don't BS you, Loki. I took you in. I took your sister in too. She didn't make it. We buried her in the sewers. But you have to survive. You're all I have. It's getting worse. We can't stick our heads in the sand. We have to face the facts. You need help. Maybe Tara's grandmother can help you."

"But this is my home," Loki said. He seemed on the verge of tears.

"I know," Aeon said, his expression grave. "I've tried to provide a home for you. Come back to it. You can come back healed."

"You could come with."

"No." Aeon turned back toward the stove and cracked an egg into the pan. "I'm too old. I would only slow you down. It takes me an hour just to get up to the upper levels with my knees the way they are. You'll have a hard enough time as it is. If you don't get caught, it will be a miracle."

"But you need my help here." A tear slid down Loki's cheek.

I turned away, studying my hands.

"I'll manage, Loki," Aeon turned back to him. "Like I did before you came to live here. Do you think I want you to leave? I wish I could keep you here with me forever. You're like my child. I know I'm not much. I'm just an old man who fixes broken things. I live in a concrete box underground. But I've tried to protect you. I've tried to keep you safe and teach you what I can. I don't want you to leave. But you need to take this chance. If someone can fix what those doctors did to you, you have to take the chance."

Loki sat, staring at his untouched food.

Aeon turned, stood looking at him for a moment, then closed the distance between them with two steps and placed his hand on Loki's shoulder. "Think about it," he said. "Go for a walk and think about it. Take your time but come back with your decision. Eat those eggs first, though, no sense wasting food."

Loki took a bite, chewing slowly, the muscles in his jaw standing out. He looked up at Aeon who was now cooking eggs for himself, back turned. "Father," Loki said. Aeon's back stiffened. "You're right. They're getting worse, my attacks. I'll go, try to get help." Loki hung his head.

Aeon turned and walked to him, placed a hand on his shoulder again. They remained frozen in that position, silent, for a long time.

ↄ৩ↄ৩

Loki and I walked side by side. We were climbing the ramps, circling around and around, heading to the ground level where we could exit. Loki was silent, brooding. I had left Xel behind with Aeon. Xel complained about it, but it wasn't safe to travel in the open with him. He was too valuable and also people would be on the lookout for a girl matching my description with a cat. Aeon had checked the news feeds and there was a reward offered for information about me. I kept my hood up and my hair tucked away. Aeon had given me sunglasses to put on when we got to the surface. I was going to wear my respie but Aeon said people didn't have them where we were going—it would be another clue that I didn't belong.

Normally, I was fine with silence. I didn't understand why people felt like they always needed to be chattering at each other. I felt nervous, though. It was weird to walk along next to a complete stranger without saying anything. I wasn't really used to being alone with a boy my age either.

"Why were you in the sewer last night?" I asked, finally.

Loki stared ahead, continuing to walk as he answered. "I was scavenging some parts. There's an old control room they don't use anymore. Lots of circuit boards."

"But how did you happen to find us?"

"Saw you in the tunnel. Heard you first, actually. I followed you. I thought the rats might come out. I waited when you went to sleep. Wanted to make sure you were okay."

I nodded, trying to think of some way to keep the conversation going. "Is your n—name really Loki?" I asked, stammering, immediately feeling like it was a stupid or possibly offensive question.

He glanced over at me, and I looked away from his face, embarrassed. He had a nice face. He was serious and didn't smile much but I was sure people would say the same thing about me.

"It's the name Aeon gave me. I don't know my real name. Or the name I was given when I was born anyway."

"Oh, right. Sorry." I was correct. It was a stupid question. I hoped he wasn't offended. "It's the name of a Norse god. We learned about him at school. Mythology," I said, feeling dumb.

"I've never been to school. I don't *think* I have anyway. I don't remember much of anything from before I came to live with Aeon."

"Nothing?"

"Just a few flashes. A hospital room. Someone's face. Way back, I remember sitting on some stairs. Wood stairs. In the sun. I was warm."

I nodded and kept walking, hurrying to keep up. Loki didn't seem used to walking with other people either. He walked fast but still with the limp I had noticed before. It felt good to stretch my legs. I had never really walked like that—striding forward, each step as long as I could make it.

The upper levels of the garage were pretty much the same as the one Loki and Aeon lived on. There were rows and rows of makeshift shelters. Some were elaborate, with vast collections of junk. Others looked newer—tucked in between older structures wherever space had been left.

There were lights on now so it wasn't as dark as it had been when we arrived the previous night. Aeon had told me they were on a timer. They turned on during the day, powered by solar panels on the top level. There were porta potties on every level and a bath house on the third floor where people could take showers. Loki and Aeon were lucky to have their own bathroom, but they still had to ration water.

They were only allowed a certain amount per day so showers had to be quick. I had taken a very short shower before we left and was feeling cleaner but still a little bewildered. I was taking it all in, trying to process the difference between how my family lived and how the people here lived. I was starting to understand that my life, as unhappy as I felt, was privileged. Still, I would rather live in a place like this, I thought, than have a mind control device in my brain. Remembering that, I peeked over at Loki. He really did have something in his brain.

"What's school like?" he asked, turning his face toward me for an instant.

"Well…" I hesitated. "I don't really like it. It's a lot of sitting still and paying attention while teachers talk. You don't have any school at all?"

"We have a daycare for little kids. After that, we apprentice with someone. Aeon teaches me about electronics. He went to college. He was an engineer a long time ago. We have a neighbor, Madeleine, who teaches me math and writing. She used to be a teacher at a school."

I nodded, not sure how to respond. "That sounds good," I said at last. "A lot of what I learn in school seems pretty useless."

We reverted to silence after that and kept walking. At the next turn, I saw daylight ahead. We were on our way to something Loki and Aeon called The Market. I wasn't sure what to expect. We had discussed Xel's plan to hop a freight train, and Aeon had agreed it was probably our best chance. Either that or stow away on one of the autotrucks that traveled in caravans on the interstates.

Aeon and Xel had come up with a list of things we would need. My purchases from the surplus store were a good start, but we would need more food, a tarp, sleeping bags, and a variety of smaller items.

The ramps kept going up, but Loki turned and led the way to a wide opening that had once been the place where cars entered and exited the garage. There were two men stationed at the entrance. Loki waved to them. There was a tall chain link gate that could be pulled across to close off the entrance but it was wide open.

"Are they guards?" I asked.

"Yes. We all take turns. We have a sort of council of volunteers who manage the community. They assign tasks. I maintain the lights. Aeon used to but he can't get up and down the ladders very well anymore."

"What are they guarding against?"

"Homeless people. Wild dogs. There are packs of dogs out here. Dangerous. Like the rats last night. They don't usually come around during the day, though."

We had seen a few people inside, many of whom had greeted Loki by name. At the gate, we met a group of men and women, all wearing corp overalls, heading off to work it seemed, and let them pass out before us.

"How do they get to work from here?" I asked.

"The train." Loki pointed. "There's a stop a couple of blocks that way."

We had emerged from the garage onto a desolate looking street lined with utility poles and stunted trees. Weeds grew up through the cracked pavement. Across the street was a five-story building stretching the full length of the block that looked like it might have been offices at one time. All the windows were either broken or boarded up. I turned and looked up. The garage also stretched up another five stories above ground. Each floor was painted a different color and there was a bright mural

showing scenes of children playing, people working in a garden, men and women dancing. The sign for the garage was painted over and incorporated into the mural but I could still make out the letters: Quik Park.

Loki saw me looking at it. "That's by Carlos. He paints murals all around the garage. We should walk the upper levels when we get back. It's nicer up there with the sunlight. The garden is nice, too, up top."

"Okay," I answered, and Loki gestured to the left.

"Market's that way."

"Where are we?" I asked as we started down the sidewalk. "I lost any sense of distance or direction while we were underground."

"Near the old airport. LAX."

We walked for a couple of blocks, passing by more derelict buildings. We came to one though that looked like it was in better repair. Most of the windows were intact, and there were solar panels on the roof. Two children were standing on a fire escape and waved to us as we passed. I waved back.

"That's the Gray Rabbit Community. It's like ours."

"Gray rabbit. Why do they call it that?"

"I don't know. We just call ours the garage, or some old timers like Aeon still call it the Quik Park." He gestured with his head. "That's the market."

We were walking alongside a patch of rubble now that looked like the remains of another building. Up ahead was a big open area enclosed with chain link fence. A familiar feeling came over me, looking out over that flat expanse. It was something I had felt often since moving to LA. The sensation was precarious, like I was on a grid of concrete just flowing out in all directions with no end. If I stood still or closed my eyes, the grid would start to tip and I would feel like I was floating into the air. Too much space. Too much distance.

We kept walking, approaching the fence, and the feeling lessened. I saw a weathered sign that said *Lot C*. Beyond the fence, as far as I could see, there were rows of tables piled with merchandise, sunshades on poles stretched above them, and people wandering up and down the rows. We entered through a gate and stopped for a moment, surveying the market.

"It used to be a parking lot for the airport," Loki said. "Now we have market here twice a week. People come from all over to sell stuff. They go to markets in other places the rest of the week. Let's go this way. Outdoor survival stuff and surplus is at the far end."

We started walking along the edge of the market, moving slowly. I saw people selling clothing, housewares, plates, cups, pot and pans, plumbing supplies, electrical supplies, toys, games, packaged food, fresh fruits and vegetables. It went on and on. All of the stuff that wasn't food was old and used, maybe salvaged from empty buildings or abandoned homes. There were food carts too parked all along the edges of the fence— tacos, instanoodles, broiled skewers of vat meat, dumplings, rice bowls.

The smells of all the foods mixing together was intoxicating. It was getting near lunch time, and the sun was beating down hot on the top of my head. We stopped at a food cart, and Loki bought two *agua frescas* which we sipped as we walked. The crowd was diverse. I saw people dressed in all kinds of ethnic costumes, people in patched and worn clothes like Loki's, people in vintage suits, corp workers in their overalls, young people in sportswear. Finally, we came to a section where outdoor survival gear was laid out on tarps. It was all similar to what I had seen at the surplus store. Loki methodically went through the merchandise and finally selected a couple of sleeping bags, a backpack, and some other equipment. He bargained with the men who sat on folding chairs and payed with a credit chip Aeon had given him. We also picked up more instafood in the form of military rations. When we had everything on the list tucked into our backpacks we wandered back over to the food carts and bought a couple of rice bowls with kimchi. We found a patch of shade and sat side by side with our backs against the fence, eating.

"Is it true that your grandmother is a doctor?" Loki asked.

"Yes. She's an Obstetrician."

"What's that?"

"A doctor who treats pregnant women and helps them give birth. She knows other doctors though. Some of them are surgeons."

"It's true. What Aeon said about my trouble." Loki halted for a moment then went on. "It's getting worse. Slowly. It takes me longer to recover now. When I have a seizure."

"I think we can find someone to help if we can get to PacNW. My grandmother lives in a place called Eugene. Used to be Oregon.

"I want to go, but I don't want to leave Aeon. He's my only family."

"I understand," I said, feeling the grid stretching out again, limitless miles of concrete, my own emptiness surging up inside of me. "I left my family too. I had to. They wanted to put one of those things in my head too."

⚜

Back at the garage, we skipped the tour of the upper levels because I was anxious to get back to Xel, and Loki was feeling tired still from the previous night. We made our way down the ramps in silence, Loki nodding and waving to the few people we saw out. When we entered Aeon's and Loki's nest, I saw Xel up on one of the workbenches with Aeon bent over him.

"What's going on? Is he damaged? What are you doing?" I called out, alarmed.

"It's okay, Tara," Xel said, lifting his head and looking over at me. "Aeon is just fitting me with some surplus equipment."

Aeon had one of Xel's paws in his hands, but I couldn't see what he was doing.

A moment later, he straightened up and took a step back. "Done. Now you can really fight rats."

"What did you do?" I asked, curious.

Xel held up a paw. "Feel," he said.

I took his paw and felt it with my fingers. Each of his toes now ended with a sharp steel claw.

"Carbon steel," Aeon said from behind me. "Front and back. I took them off an old T-Eighty-Nine skeleton I had in the back."

"Amazing," I said, feeling the claws on his other paw. "Xel, you're ready for anything now."

"I will at least be able to protect you more effectively," he answered with a slow blink.

"You're already an expert at that," I said, hugging him. "But I'm glad you got your claws. I always felt like you should have them."

છ9છ9

Aeon fixed a big dinner that night with Loki's help. We had sausages, carrots, brussel sprouts, and potatoes from the garden up top, all roasted with spices and seasonings. Aeon said the sausage was insect protein, but it tasted good. I hadn't had a real dinner in so long I had forgotten what it was like. It was somber, though. Nobody did much talking. Aeon and Loki circled around the kitchen like gears in a machine, preparing the meal. I could tell they were used to cooking together. They were a good team. We were planning on leaving the next morning though, and they were careful with each other. It seemed like they were both processing it in their own solitary way, unfamiliar or unpracticed in expressing their love to each other. Watching them reminded me of the way my parents interacted. Probably the way I interacted with them too. We were all hard edged, closed off, solitary. It was weird to see it from the outside.

After dinner, we washed the dishes and put them away. With the last glass placed on the shelf above the sink, Aeon turned to us.

"Long day," he said. "You two should get to bed. Start of a tough journey tomorrow. I'm off to bed too. I'll wake you early."

Loki stood, looking down at his feet, nodding.

"See you in the morning." Aeon shuffled off.

"Going to bed too. See you in the morning," Loki said to me.

"Okay," I answered. He started to turn away and on impulse I spoke. "Are you okay?" I asked. "I know this is hard."

"It'll be all right," he said, voice low. "I'll come back. I owe him that."

CHAPTER 9

Setting Out

I woke up to the feeling of Xel prodding me in the side with a paw and sat up, trying to figure out where I was.

"Tara. It's time to get up."

I rubbed my eyes and looked around. The room was mostly dark with only one light on in the kitchen turned down to a honey-colored glow. I lay still for a few minutes, almost falling back to sleep but soon Aeon came in, wearing the tattered robe and pajamas I had seen him in the night we met.

He turned up the lights in the kitchen and glanced over. "Ah good. You're awake. I'm just going to put on some water to boil then wake up Loki. We can have some breakfast before you set out."

Aeon and Loki had an old gas stove in the corner converted to run on propane. Aeon lit a burner, put the kettle on, then crossed the room, and went out through the doorway into the workshop. I looked down at Xel who was crouching on the floor next to the couch.

"Are we really doing this, Xel?" I asked.

He looked back at me. "It seems like the best plan. We were fortunate to meet Loki and Aeon. We would not be well prepared without their help. Aeon has loaded detailed maps of the sewers and subway tunnels into my memory."

"I hope we make it. We are going to make it, aren't we?"

"I hope so. At least I think I hope so." Xel seemed to be pondering something. "Previously, I knew the definition of the word hope. Now I think I might feel the actual feeling. A sort of striving or yearning toward an uncertain goal. I picture the desired outcome and feel an internal stretching toward it."

"Yes," I answered. "That sounds like hope."

Half an hour later we were all sitting down to a breakfast of eggs with leftover potatoes and sausage from the night before. The breakfast was delicious but I had a hard time enjoying it. Trepidation about the journey we were embarking on was roiling my stomach. It was different when Xel and I had run away. It was just the two of us, and we were reacting to everything in the moment. Now there would be three of us. I didn't know how we would even make it two miles let alone nine hundred. The security forces were looking for me. Who knew what they would do with Loki. It seemed like a long shot. My only alternative was returning home though and facing my parents—maybe being forced into having a device in my head.

Loki and Aeon were acting gruff with each other. Watching them, I felt like an interloper who had come to break up their happy home. In fact, I was offering them a possible cure for Loki's sickness, and they were offering me much needed help and support. It was a good deal for everybody. Emotion always got in the way and made people act in irrational ways, though. It definitely happened to me sometimes, and I could see it with them.

"So, your plan is to take the Central Outfall to the East Central Interceptor and from there to the subway tunnels downtown? Then hop a freight train?" Aeon was asking Xel as much as anybody else.

"I have considered all possible routes and this seems best," Xel answered. "Staying below ground is the best option, I think. There will be much less possibility of detection by the authorities."

"Loki hasn't been that far in the sewers. We don't know what you'll find. Some weird people wandering around down there."

"I guess we'll find out," Loki said.

"Yes, you will," Aeon answered, giving him a hard look.

Finally, breakfast was over. It was six a.m., and we had our backpacks ready to go by the door. We wanted to get away before other inhabitants of the garage started to stir. The less people who saw us leaving, the better. I shouldered my backpack. Loki was puttering around, fiddling with the straps and ties on his pack. Aeon was standing nearby, seeming smaller and more frail. Thanking people was not natural for me. I somehow almost always forgot to do it. My mother was constantly reminding me. Maybe it was part of my general trouble with theory of mind, as Dr. Gutierrez had called it. That meant trying to understand what other people were thinking and feeling. I felt the impulse right then though so I stepped forward.

"Aeon, I want to thank you for taking us in and letting us stay here for the last couple of days. We really appreciate it."

"It was my pleasure. If you can get Loki the help he needs, you will be repaying me a hundred times over."

"I hope we can," I said. "We'll just step outside now and let you and Loki say goodbye. Come on, Xel." With that, I turned but Aeon spoke again and I turned back.

"Wait. Before you go. I have a present for you." He reached into the cargo pocket of his pants and pulled out something I had seen only a few times before—a paper book. "You mentioned that you like science fiction," he said, holding it out to me. "Maybe you can read this in whatever moments you have."

I took it from him, marveling at it. The library at my old school had a glass case full of old books but I had never held one in my hands.

"Thank you," I said again. "I will."

Head down then I went out with Xel on my heels. I closed the door behind me and stood with my back to it, peering out into the dark garage. Xel sat at my feet, leaning against my leg. Off and on since I made the decision to run, I had experienced moments of clarity when the absurdity of what I was doing seemed overwhelming. Just then, in the dark, with my back against the door, I felt it strongly. My pulse began to race, and I felt the itchy sensation of sweat breaking out on my forehead and under my arms. I crouched down and took deep breaths, letting my head hang.

"Are you okay, Tara?" Xel asked.

I nodded yes and continued to take deep breaths. Calmed down, the panic attack averted, I stood back up, a little shaky. A moment later, the door opened and Loki stepped out.

"Let's go," he said, averting his face and striding forward.

I stood there for a few moments, my brain saying go but my body not responding. Then, suddenly, I came unstuck and took a step, another. Xel and I followed Loki into the darkness. He turned his lantern on to a barely perceptible glow and held it out for us to follow. He was walking even faster than usual though, and I couldn't keep up in the dark.

"Loki," I whispered, "Slow down. I can't go that fast."

He stopped and waited for me to catch up. "Sorry," he whispered back then turned and kept walking but at a slower pace.

We came to the door we had passed through on the night Loki saved us from the rats. Loki opened it, stood aside as Xel and I walked through, then closed it softly. Without looking back, he started down the stairs, turning the lantern up now so that it cast a brighter glow on the damp, water stained and graffitied walls. At the bottom, we retraced our steps down the long corridor and emerged into the sewer. Black water flowed slowly below us, the lantern light glinting off its surface. I was glad I couldn't see it more clearly. I dug out my respie, holding my breath. Loki had brought along an old respie too.

"You lead the way, Xel," I said.

His eyes flashed at me in the dark and he bowed his head in a nod. "This is the Central Outfall Sewer. We will have to walk along the open sewer for approximately sixteen kilometers. It's a full day of walking. We should try to get to the East Central Interceptor by evening so we can get away from the raw sewage. This way." Xel turned left and began walking. Loki followed, and I brought up the rear.

We walked for all of that day along the narrow path underground with the dark water sliding along beside us. I saw rats occasionally but only in ones and twos. They ignored us, scuttling along on their own business. I saw lots of cockroaches too. The first couple of times I jumped, letting out a gasp. After that, I just took them for part of the landscape and ignored the peripheral glints of

lantern light on their shiny bodies as they scurried across
the walls. Sometimes I would see things float by in the
water too—mysterious, dark shapes, nothing I could easily recognize.

The walls themselves and the floor below us shifted
from concrete to brick and back again as we passed
through older and newer sections of the sewer. In some
old sections yellow stalactites hung down from the ceiling, built up by years of water seeping down through the
cracks in the brick and depositing minerals. In some places, near where ladders ran up to manholes high above, we
saw graffiti and empty spray paint cans. We didn't see
any other people though. It was quiet and monotonous.
By mid-day, my legs and feet ached. We stopped periodi-
cally to drink water or a quick liquid nutrient pack but
neither of us wanted to keep our respies off for long. The
air was rancid and moist. It was all I could do to suck
down a few quick sips of water or nutrients without becoming nauseated.

I kept my hoodie on despite the warmth, not wanting
too much of my skin exposed to the air. Xel set the pace,
staying in the lead. He walked slower probably than Loki
would have liked, but I was glad. Xel was looking out for
me. I wasn't in great shape and the exertions of the last
few days had made my body sore and tired. Sometimes
Xel would stop, sniffing the air for a few moments before
continuing. I made a mental note to ask him whether he
could separate out the stench of the sewage enough to
really smell anything else. I knew he must be able to but I
couldn't imagine it.

As the day wore on and we continued walking in silence, I started to feel more and more how strange it was
to be traveling with someone who was an almost-total
stranger. In our short time together, Xel and I had formed
a bond. Xel's programming was written with exactly this

purpose in mind. In military situations, special operations soldiers would be assigned a companion like Xel when they were sent on solitary missions. They would become a team, learning from each other, able to anticipate each other's movements and reactions. Loki was quiet and reticent and so was I.

We had begun to get to know each other a little, but we were still strangers. I didn't really know how to become someone's friend. I had only done it once in my life and all the effort had been Rosie's. I still didn't know why Rosie had chosen me that first day in fourth grade when she had walked up to me on the playground and asked if I wanted to help her dig. We spent that recess digging holes around the roots of a tree, lining them with grass, and gathering stones and nuts to decorate them with. We had been friends ever since. Now, on the run, in the sewers below Los Angeles, our group of three felt off balance, without enough shared experiences and knowledge to be comfortable together. I was used to being uncomfortable around other people. This felt different, though. We were on this journey together. It was awkward.

I knew Loki must be feeling a lot of emotion too, bottling it up. There was no chance to talk though, with our respies on, traveling through that weird, quiet underworld. Getting to know each other would have to wait.

Finally, in the afternoon, we came to the place Xel had been leading us to. There was a smaller tunnel that branched off at an angle, leading upward at a slight grade. It had no walkway so we had to climb down, careful to avoid the sewage flowing by, and walk carefully along the curved, dry bottom. After only a few minutes of walking, we emerged into a larger tunnel again that was much like the one Xel and I had originally found, with the same sort of catwalk.

"This is the East Central Interceptor," Xel said. "We made it. I suggest continuing a bit farther then stopping for the night. I can see that you are both tired."

Xel was right, I was dead tired, but I wanted to get away from the stench of the sewage so I agreed. Loki had to help me up to the catwalk. He scrambled up first then reached a hand down for me. When our fingers touched, I felt a shiver run through me at the contact. Touching other people was a little weird for me. He didn't seem to notice, though. His hand was strong and callused. He pulled me up, and I was able to get a leg over the edge of the catwalk, a hand on the rail. My sore muscles protested, but I pulled myself up from there.

We marched along for another twenty minutes before we came to an alcove like the one Xel and I had stopped in before. We all looked at each other and came to a mutual, wordless decision to stop there. I dropped to the floor, back to the wall, hugging my knees with my arms. For a minute, I just sat there, overjoyed to be done walking. Xel lay down, curled up next to me. After a while, I realized I could probably take my respie off. I lifted it over my head and sniffed the air. It was dank but not nauseating. Loki, sitting across from me with his back to the other wall of the alcove, also took his respie off, breathed deeply, and exhaled.

"That was a walk," he said

"Yeah. I'm exhausted," I replied.

"Hungry?" he asked and I nodded yes.

He opened his backpack and got out two instafood meal packs, two forks. There was a water tap just like in the other alcove where Xel and I had stopped so I refilled both of our water bottles and passed Loki's back to him. We sat and ate in silence then. Despite my aversion to instafood, I ate every morsel. I even ran my finger around the inside of the biodegradable container to get the last

few crumbs. I wasn't used to physical exertion and the
hunger that came along with it. I had never been athletic
or even active. I preferred to sit and read a book. My parents were the same way. I hadn't ever thought about it,
but maybe I was that way because they were. Maybe I
had never been shown any other way to be. I was sore
and tired but it felt kind of good actually. It felt rewarding
to have done something difficult and then to rest.

After we finished our food, we sat for a while in silence, just resting. The lantern was on the ground between us, creating a comforting circle of light in the dark.
I was beginning to feel sleepy, my eyes drooping, when
Loki stretched, stood, and began to dig in his pack.

"We should put up the tent," he said. "We don't want
to get caught out if the rats show up again."

I stood too and helped as best I could. Working together, it didn't take long. The tent just fit between the
back wall of the alcove and the railing of the catwalk. It
was made of an extremely light and tough carbon nano
fabric that would keep out any unwanted visitors. We put
our backpacks inside, crawled in, and laid out our sleeping bags. The tent was big enough for us to lay side by
side, propped up on our packs with the lantern between
us. We left the tent door unzipped and Xel stationed himself there, sitting with his back to us, guarding. Loki was
digging in his pack again. I looked over and saw him take
out a small bamboo flute.

"Do you mind if I play?" he asked, eyes on the roof
of the tent.

"No. I mean yes, please—go ahead," I stammered.

He lifted the flute and took a deep breath. The first
note was low and long, dying out to silence at the end.
Another long note, higher, trembling followed, then a
slow arpeggio first up, then down. His playing went on
like that, slow and meditative. I closed my eyes and lis-

tened, forgetting for a little while where we were and why we were there. He must have played for twenty minutes. The last note was like the first, dying out so slowly it was hard to tell when it ended. I opened my eyes and looked over at him. Xel had turned and his face was lifted, eyes closed.

"I think, perhaps, that was beautiful music," Xel said softly. "I am unsure. The experience of beauty is new to me."

"Yes, it was," I said. "Very beautiful. What kind of instrument is that?"

Loki held it up. "Shakuhachi," he said. "A meditation flute. Aeon gave it to me before we left. It's his own flute. He taught me to play. It helps me relax sometimes when I feel an episode coming. Are you going to read the book? The one Aeon gave you?"

"Yes," I said. I had almost forgotten about it. "Do you want me to read it aloud?"

He nodded, still looking up at the ceiling of the tent. I found it in my pack, settled myself, and opened the book carefully. It was old and the pages were yellowed and brittle. I had never read a paper book, but I knew how they were supposed to work. Printed text on paper was a lot different than the words that hung in front of my vision when I read books on my specs. Slowly, I turned the pages until I came to chapter one, then cleared my throat and began.

"'Two pieces of yesterday were in Captain Davidson's mind when he woke...'"

∽∽∽

I woke disoriented the next morning but recovered quickly. My body was a different story though. I tried to sit up and every muscle complained at the movement.

Still, I pushed myself up and turned the lantern on low. Xel was seated in the tent opening. Loki was still asleep.

"Good morning, Tara."

"Morning, Xel. What time is it?"

"Six forty-three," he said.

I nodded, yawned, rubbed my eyes. "How far do we have to go today?"

"Approximately the same distance as yesterday. We should try to be up and moving by eight at the latest."

"Okay," I said, laying back. "I'm just going to rest a little bit longer."

When I woke again, Loki was up, stuffing his rolled sleeping bag into his pack.

I sat up. "What time is it now?"

"Seven thirty-four," Xel answered.

"We should get going pretty soon," Loki said.

"Okay. I'm up," I answered.

I turned and dug a breakfast packet out of my pack, dumped the powder into my water bottle, and drank it down in a few gulps. I needed to pee so I put my boots on and walked a ways down the tunnel. By the time I got back, the tent was broken down and packed away. I stretched for a minute, trying to remember the warm-up exercises we had run through in gym class at PVCSTEM. I was sure I looked stupid but I felt a little better by the time I was done. I heaved my pack up onto my back and adjusted the straps.

"Ready," I said.

Loki nodded and gestured to Xel to lead us.

We spent the morning walking at a fairly slow pace. I had broken down and told Xel and Loki how sore I was from the previous day, explaining that I didn't get much exercise, especially since my family moved. Back in PacNW, I at least walked half a mile each way to school and back, rode bikes with Rosie, ran around during gym

class. The walking was less unpleasant. We didn't have
to wear respies, and there was no raw sewage. Around
midday, we stopped for a break. Shortly after we got going again though, Xel stopped abruptly, turning his ears
and sniffing.

"What is it?" I whispered.

"Something ahead," he answered. "I thought I heard
a voice, a child crying. A sound of metal on metal. I
smell food cooking."

Loki and I looked at each other.

"Could be a camp," he said. "I've heard of people
living in the sewers, if they don't have anywhere else to
go."

"What do we do?"

"Go on ahead, I guess. If it is a camp, we just walk
by, hope they leave us alone. I have this—" He pulled out
a small device from his pocket and held it up. "—in case
anybody tries to stop us."

"What is it?"

"A taser. Shocks people. It won't hurt them, just
immobilize them for a little while."

"Okay," I said, feeling nervous.

"Just keep walking. Don't look at anything. Try to
seem calm."

I nodded, and we all turned and began walking again.
Xel stayed close to my side and Loki walked a little bit in
front. The tunnel curved to the right ahead. As we rounded the turn, I saw light and smelled smoke. We continued
walking and the patch of light grew closer. I began to
make out shapes. There were several temporary shelters
like the ones in the garage but much less elaborate—just
sheets of plastic. A woman was seated in the middle of
the spillway on a plastic box, tending a small grill. Smoke
rose from the grill and floated down the tunnel in our direction. A large man stood a few paces behind the wom-

an. He was looking our way. As we approached a young child came out of one of the shelters followed by an older boy who must have been fifteen or sixteen years old. They all watched us as we moved closer, looking up toward the catwalk.

As we drew even with them, the child ran to the woman and wrapped its arms around her, looking back at us through an unkempt mop of brown hair. The teenager and the man both stared at us, mouths open. I took one glance back as we passed and saw the man looking over at the boy.

He said something—a surprising sound in that silent place. I didn't understand the language. It sounded like grunting. They both stepped forward still watching us then began to walk then to jog toward us.

"Run," Xel said. "I will bring up the rear."

Loki and I began running along the catwalk. The lantern bounced in Loki's grasp, casting crazy dancing shadows on the walls. Xel loped along behind. I couldn't go very quickly on the catwalk with the backpack. My muscles ached with the effort, my pulse beat fast with fear, and perspiration slid down my forehead. I kept running, feet clanking on the metal below. Loki glanced back.

"Faster," he said. "They're catching up."

I heard the man yelling in the darkness behind us. He sounded angry. I tried to run faster, but I could feel that they were gaining.

Suddenly, Xel let out a fearsome hiss. I turned just in time to see the man jump up, grasp the struts, and try to raise himself to the catwalk. Xel was there, though, with claws flashing in the lantern light. Bloody tracks were drawn across the man's arm and face. I saw his mouth open in surprise and pain, his gums toothless, as he fell back.

The boy was also climbing up. Loki stepped forward, and I saw a flash as the taser arced, and the boy fell back too.

"Forward. Another twenty meters. Doorway on the left," Xel said.

We all started running. I heard the man and the boy yelling again, back on our trail. Loki was in the lead. Just as Xel had said, there was an alcove ahead and a door. Loki pulled his keychain out of his pocket and slid a key into the lock.

"Master key," he said as he turned it and pushed the door open.

I slipped through followed by Xel and then Loki who slammed the steel door closed. A moment later there came a loud bang as the man threw his shoulder against the door.

"Let's go," Xel said. "It is improbable that he will succeed in breaking down the door, but we should move away just in case."

I looked around, panting, trying to get my breath back. We were in a narrow tunnel with an arched roof.

"Lead the way," Loki answered.

Xel turned and led us along the tunnel at a quick trot. My lungs burned and I had a stitch in my side but I kept up. The sound of the man banging against the door followed us down the corridor, growing softer as we continued. After twenty minutes, we came to a wider area where there was a short flight of steps leading up and another tunnel branching off the right.

"I need to rest," I said between gasps and leaned against the wall, holding my sides.

"Okay. Let's stop here for a minute," Loki said and sat down with his back to the wall. He was winded too.

Xel stood facing the direction from which we had come. He emitted a low growl, then turned and spoke. "I no longer hear banging. I think they have given up. We will not be able to go back that way, though, unless we want to face them again and maybe others. Are you both okay?"

"Yes, fine," Loki answered and I nodded yes.

"Where does this tunnel go?" Loki asked.

"If we take this side tunnel, it will lead us to the Los Angeles River. We could travel up the river to the I-Five freeway and attempt to stow away on a caravan. It was my secondary plan, if the sewer didn't work out."

"All right," I said. "Let's do it."

Loki and I stood and we set off again. None of us wanted to stick around that place. I thought of the man's face, his angry voice, and the banging of his shoulder against the door. I didn't want to be around if he got through the door and came after us.

Half an hour later, we came to a stairway leading up. It was long and my legs were shaking by the time we got to the top. There was a landing and an old steel door hanging on its hinges, daylight bleeding in around the edges. I squinted my eyes. The light was dazzlingly bright after so long in the darkness underground. Xel shouldered the door open and walked out. Loki and I followed and stood in the doorway, shading our eyes with our hands. Before us was a massive concrete basin almost a hundred yards across. It was flat on the bottom with sloping walls. The doorway we stood in was near the top of the slope.

A trickle of water, scummed with algae, ran down the center and weeds and grass grew from cracks in the concrete. Looking upriver, I saw a freeway overpass crossing high above the basin. On the far side was a chain link fence fallen over in places. Beyond that were old warehouses and factory buildings. I looked over at Loki and his eyes were distant, his face blank. Suddenly his pupils rolled up and his body went slack.

I managed to keep his head from hitting the ground, catching him just in time and kneeling with his head on my lap. His body was rigid and shaking. All I could do was sit there, hands on either side of his head, feeling the tremors run through him, hoping he would be all right.

CHAPTER 10

The River

When Loki's seizure finally ended, I left him lying by himself for a few minutes while I unpacked the tent and set it up just inside the doorway on the landing. The day was warm and humid but the shade inside gave some relief and protection from the sun. I stretched out Loki's sleeping bag inside the tent and went out to where he lay. Xel nudged his head under Loki's shoulder, helping him sit up, and I helped him from there to his hands and knees. I felt his tense muscles through his T-shirt and once again a shiver ran through me just as it had when I touched his hand the day before. I felt an urge to draw away but, at the same time, a desire to leave my hand where it was—to maintain the contact. It was not like anything I had felt before. Almost always in the past, physical contact with another person, especially a stranger, would make me recoil. What was it about Loki, I wondered, that made him different? I distrusted myself. Sometimes I felt things too strongly—like a wild wind sweeping through my mind and body. In the moment, I couldn't put a name to the emotion. Later when I had time to think it through, I could untangle it and figure it out. I would have to think about it later.

Once Loki was in the tent and laying down with his water bottle beside him, drifting off into a fitful sleep, I went back to the doorway where Xel was gazing out at the river and sat down next to him. My legs dangled over the edge of the platform, and I kicked the cement with my heels.

"When you said river, I didn't picture this."

"Yes," Xel answered. "Rivers are normally more natural. The LA River was diverted into this concrete channel in the twentieth century to decrease flooding. There are some stretches where the concrete was removed and the river was allowed to return to a more natural state. We will pass through one of those on our way."

I nodded, thinking. "What should we do Xel?" I asked softly.

"Loki needs to rest. We can stay here and resume our journey tomorrow."

"Do you think he'll be all right?"

"We need to get him to your grandmother. He needs medical attention."

"I know." I paused for a moment, feeling overwhelmed. "I miss my mom, Xel," I said. "And my dad. I miss having adults to tell me what to do. I don't know if I'm strong enough to do this."

"You are strong enough, Tara. I believe in you."

"Thanks, Xel. I hope you're right."

છજછ

Loki woke up around five p.m. and I made us an instafood dinner. We ate sitting cross-legged in the tent.

""'I'm sorry," Loki said, between bites, eyes downcast.

"It's okay. It's not your fault. Without you, those people in the sewer would have caught me."

"It was the taser," he said, still not looking at me. "I've never used it before. It made me feel sick, shocking that boy with it."

"I understand. You did what you had to."

"Yeah. I guess so. It didn't feel good, though."

I felt the urge to reach out, touch his arm. I didn't though. My hand stayed on my lap. "I hope we don't have any more situations like that," I said finally. "I was scared."

"Yeah. Me too," he answered.

Loki played his flute for us again and, afterward, I read more of Aeon's book aloud. Xel listened attentively to my reading.

"Are you enjoying the book?" I asked him.

"Yes," he answered. "I am able to access the net now that we are above ground, but I have decided not to download a synopsis of the plot. I find that it is pleasurable to anticipate the story. There are many possibilities. Some possibilities I favor. Others I do not. I feel mild anxiety about how the plot will unfold. Is this what people enjoy about literature?"

"Yeah, I think so," Loki answered. "Although some people enjoy the way the story is told more than the story itself. Aeon says he likes to read for the beauty of the writing. I like to read more for the story."

"I think I like both," I said.

"I understand," Xel said. "I will pay more attention to the artistry of the language. Perhaps that is also something I will enjoy. Please continue."

It was almost peaceful there by the river. Occasionally, we would hear a floater buzzing by in the distance.

Once, we saw a lone figure trudging by on the far side of the basin. He was pushing a cart loaded with junk and didn't seem to notice us. Los Angeles had once been a crowded, densely populated city. Now, only pockets were populated. Playa Vista, where my family lived and the corporations were in control was one pocket. Santa Monica was another. Downtown was another. The in-between space, I was learning, was mostly empty, the buildings and streets crumbling.

Around eight p.m., Loki drifted off while I was reading. I was sleepy too so I put the book away and lay down. My mind wandered, slowly winding down toward sleep. I thought about how I hadn't worn my specs for several days. Except at school, I didn't even remember the last time I went for a few hours, let alone a full day without them on. Specs were just a day-to-day necessity, or so I had thought. Now, I realized that it was mainly true for people in the corp enclaves. I had seen lots of people who lived without them at the garage. Aeon and Loki only used them when they needed to download some information. They were less common in PacNW but still, most people had them. Without them, my mind felt clearer, calmer. I felt like I could focus better. I was noticing new things. Maybe I would stick to not using them, or only when I really needed to, I thought as I drifted off. If only we could make it to PacNW safely.

⚬⚬⚬

We packed up and left early the next morning. Along both sides of the river there were flat walking paths but Xel thought it would be better for us to stay down in the spillway. That way, we would not be seen from ground level unless somebody was looking down into the basin from the edge. Loki and I agreed so we climbed down carefully and set out from there. The cement was cracked and crumbling under my fingers as I backed down the slope, using my hands to keep my balance with the heavy pack on my back. Xel didn't like us being so exposed to surveillance from above but he had checked the news feeds, and it didn't seem that the search was still active. They were still on the lookout for me and a reward was offered, but the security forces were not combing the city by floater as they had been the day I escaped from the hospital. Still, Xel stayed some distance apart from us, keeping to the long grasses and weeds that grew in the center of the basin. He darted from one clump of vegetation to the next and stayed mostly hidden.

For Loki and me, it was hot and dusty walking. I asked Xel around mid-morning and he told me it was ninety-two degrees. We drank a lot of water. Luckily, Loki had purchased a surplus filter at the market so we were able to fill our bottles from the small, dirty stream that flowed down the center of the spillway. I used an extra T-shirt to cover my head and neck and protect my skin from the sun. As we walked, we passed under lots of bridges and overpasses. Sometimes we saw people or vehicles above but they did not seem interested in us. It was a relief to get a brief respite from the sun when we passed into the shade cast by one of the overhead structures. Around midday, we stopped in the shade below a curving overpass to rest and eat. I sat down on my pack, pulled off my boots and socks, then carefully made my way to the water, wincing when I stepped on rocks and bits of debris. When I reached the river, I sat on a big piece of broken concrete and dunked both feet. The water was not cold, but still it felt good on my overheated skin. My feet looked yellow brown below the surface of the silty water. In the center of the stream, almost rusted away, was an old shopping cart laying on its side. I watched the water flow over and through it. Algae clung to the wire and waved in the current.

"Careful. There's a lot of junk under that water. Could be something sharp," Loki called to me.

"I know," I answered. "I'm being careful."

Just after that stop we came to a stretch where the basin widened and the walls on either side became much steeper. The water that had flowed down the center was spread thin across the surface so that we had to walk through it between islands of dry concrete and drifted mounds of dirt and garbage. A great flock of seagulls were scattered about in the water and lifted up, swirling into the sky, as we trudged through their midst. On the bank to our left, beyond a cyclone fence, were the hulking remains of giant storage tanks and pipes. Maybe some kind of refinery or treatment facility.

Shortly after that, we came to a stretch where the concrete bed of the river dropped away and was replaced by sand, rock, and thriving vegetation. Trees grew up on the banks of the river and the water collected in still, deep pools. Looking into the depths, I thought I saw the shiny silver back of a fish dart past. It was a relief to be under the shade of the trees and the air seemed cooler, but it was also slower going, scrambling through underbrush, over tree roots and boulders, sometimes wading through shallow parts of the river itself.

By late afternoon, we were approaching the end of this natural part of the river. I could see up ahead another section of concrete, shivering in the haze of rising heat.

"What time is it, Xel?" I asked.

"Almost five p.m."

"I think we should stop here for the day."

Loki came up beside me, nodding his agreement. "This is a good place to camp," he said. "Under the trees instead of out in the open."

We put up the tent after we ate but it was so warm out, even after dark, that we decided to lay down our tarp and put our sleeping bags on the ground outside. Laying there, under the night sky, we gazed out at the bright stars. I couldn't remember ever being outside, at night, lying down and looking up like that. It felt weird and exhilarating, like I could feel the earth spinning under me, and I might fly off.

"Aeon told me Los Angeles used to be so bright that you could barely see the stars at night," Loki said.

"That is true," Xel answered. He was sitting next to me, also looking up at the stars. "It was called light pollution. Many millions of people lived here. Public spaces were lit at all times. The lights were overly bright and highly inefficient."

"I guess at least we fixed that problem," Loki said, sounding bitter. "From what I've heard, it was better back then for people like me, though. You couldn't just take people and do experiments on them then dump them and hope they died."

"Yes," Xel answered. "At least in this part of North America. Other places were just as bad."

"Why did they want to put the thing in your head?" Loki asked suddenly, turning his head toward me.

I kept looking at the stars, thinking. Finally, I answered. "The doctors said my brain didn't work right somehow. They said I could be more social and have friends and understand other people better. I've been thinking about what they said, ever since I ran away. Sometimes I think they were right, at least partially. I am pretty weird."

Loki nodded, looking back up at the sky. "Being weird is okay," he said after a while. "I like you the way you are."

"So do I," Xel said.

"Thanks," I answered.

Laying there with Loki and Xel, looking up at the stars, I felt—for a few minutes at least—like I had made the right decision, like running away from my family and home was worth it.

൞൞൞

The next morning we set off again, upriver, leaving the trees and deep pools behind. We were traveling in the concrete basin again with the scorching sun on our faces. As we closed in on downtown, there were even more bridges and overpasses than before. There was fresher garbage and graffiti too. A couple of times we saw make-shift structures under the bridges and passed by quickly, giving them a wide berth. We didn't see any other people, though.

Near mid-day, we passed the remains of an automobile that had been driven or pushed down into the riverway. It was rusted and the window glass was all broken. Inside, I could see the steering wheel and the seat where the driver would have sat. The front wheels had sunk into the center channel, and the water flowed around it. Tall weeds grew up out of the engine compartment.

"Old one," Loki said. "It's the kind of car you could operate manually."

"Yeah, I've seen them before." I answered. "Some people still have them in the Pacific Northwest Cluster."

"Ever ridden in one?"

"No. Can you imagine? They used to go a hundred miles an hour. People used to crash them into each other and die. They were powered by burning fossil fuel and pumping the smoke into the air. I'd much rather have a computer drive me."

"I've never been in a car at all. Except maybe before,

the time I can't remember. And the one that dropped me off when Aeon found me."

I nodded, not sure what to say. We looked at the car for a while longer, marveling at the old technology, then turned away and continued walking.

I was finally over being stiff and sore, and my body was beginning to feel good. I was developing muscles in my legs from the days of walking and running. I felt something I had never felt before—strong, and capable. I could walk all day now. I was still tired, my feet still hurt at the end of the day, and I knew I could be in a lot better shape, but it felt good. Loki looked better too. Being out in the sun and exercising was good for both of us.

Finally, early in the afternoon, we came to a massive freeway interchange. Giant overpasses crossed above our heads, some intersecting, some higher some lower. We could hear the big trucks driving on them. Pigeons roosted in the steel girders that held all that concrete up in the air and the ground was littered with their poop and feathers.

"That's the interstate," Xel said, gesturing with his head toward the largest of the freeways. "Near here there is a staging yard where the autotrucks drop off trailers and pick up new ones. We will need to leave the river and get to the staging yard. There we can find a trailer bound north and hide inside it."

"How are we going to manage that?" I asked.

"We will have adjust our plan as we go," Xel answered, "depending on the conditions. We should rest here and go after dark."

We spent the rest of the day resting in the shade of the freeway interchange. Xel prowled off by himself for a while, checking out the surroundings and scoping out the freight yard.

He returned around dusk.

Loki and I were just finishing our dinner of instafood loaf and dried fruit and nut mix.

"I located a container that will be leaving tonight, heading north," he said. "It contains shoes manufactured in Thailand and is going to the BC Cluster. It is not full so we should be able to fit. We can slip into the yard sometime after nightfall. There is a place just there—" He gestured with a paw. "—where we can get through the fence to leave the river. We will then need to cross a road that seems seldom used and climb a wall to gain access to the freight yard."

"How do you know all of this?" Loki asked.

"I accessed the freight company's data systems while I was performing my reconnaissance."

"I thought your programming kept you from hacking," I said, alarmed. "You're not supposed to be able to do anything illegal."

"Yes. It is supposed to. However, I find that my deepening ability to feel emotion has overridden that programming. Perhaps in the same way that humans often disregard laws they would otherwise obey when they are under emotional duress. Also, their security was quite poor. Accessing their data was trivial."

"I guess I know why they were so upset by the changes I made to your firmware," I said. "But I'm glad I did."

We watched the sun go down behind the towering buildings of the Los Angeles city core then waited another hour before setting out. It didn't take long to cross over the stream and scramble up the opposite bank. At the top, we found the hole in the fence Xel had passed through earlier. Xel went through then Loki. I stopped for a moment, looking back at the massive concrete basin, silvery in the moonlight that glinted off the trickle of water in the middle, and gave thanks to that river for allowing us to travel with it for a stretch and for keeping us safe. With one last look back, I ducked and squeezed through the opening in the fence.

On the other side was a garbage-strewn no man's land of gravel and concrete, a barricade which we climbed over, and then a four-lane road. Fifty meters down the road, an autotruck was just pulling out, passing through an armed gate. We watched it go by. The front end was a curved, aerodynamic surface studded with the sensors the computer used to pilot the truck. After it passed, we darted across the road and found ourselves at the base of a wall about three meters high and topped with razor wire. Xel motioned for us to turn right and follow. He led us away from the gate along the perimeter of the fence. After about a hundred paces, he stopped, looking up toward the top of the wall. I looked up too, following his gaze. There was a dirty blanket thrown over the razor wire and under it, propped against the wall, was a pallet.

"Somebody else entered here," Xel said. "This is how I got in earlier. You will have to climb to the top of the pallet and pull yourselves up from there. The blanket is thick and will protect you from the wire. Drop down on the far side."

Loki nodded to me. "You first," he said. "I can give you a push to help you over."

I climbed up the pallet so that my toes were on the upper edge and wrapped my fingers over the top of the wall. Loki got behind me, put his hands under my heels, counted to three, then shoved as I jumped. I lifted a foot and scrambled up, careful not to cut myself on the bits of razor that poked through the blanket. I eased myself over the other side, lowered myself to hanging, took a deep breath, and let go. For an instant, I was hanging in the air, then I hit the ground with a jarring thud and rolled over backward. By the time I regained my feet, Loki was hanging and dropping, landing next to me and rolling over too. Xel bounded over the wall and landed gracefully next to us. He stood for a moment, absolutely still, ears rotated outward.

"Dogs," he said, "coming this way. Follow me quickly."

He turned to the right and began to run. Loki and I followed. To my right was the wall we had come over. To my left, rows and rows of steel cargo containers flashing by as we ran. Suddenly, Xel turned, dashing down one of the rows, and we followed. The containers were big—three meters high and four times as long. I heard something behind us and glanced back. Two bounding figures were following and gaining on us.

"Here. Climb to the top!" Xel cried as he wheeled and faced the dogs. I scrambled up the steel rungs welded to the exterior of the container and Loki followed on my heels. Below I heard a yelp, a hiss, and a sound of tearing. I threw myself onto the top of the container and crawled to the edge. Below, I saw Xel moving like a whirlwind. One of the dogs was already down. The other was fighting, but it was no match for Xel. He was on its back in an instant, claws tearing it apart. A moment later, he was dragging the dog parts into the shadows between two other containers. Loki joined me but there was nothing else to see. Xel emerged from the shadows and followed us up to the top of the container. I turned and sat, facing him, the steel cool and damp underneath me.

"What happened? Were those robot dogs?"

"Primitive brains. Not AI. I dispatched them."

"What if they did have brains? What would you do?"

"I don't know, Tara. My primary mission is to protect you. I would not like to kill another AI that could think and feel. I probably would if I had to. Let's get inside. This container is scheduled to be shipped out in less than an hour."

There was a locked hatch on the top of the container. I got out my plasma knife while Loki and Xel moved to stand between me and a distant tower where workers dispatched cranes to move containers on and off of waiting trucks. Hoping they would block out enough of the light and sparks to keep from drawing the attention of the tower, I flipped the knife on and hastily cut through the lock. We entered the container quickly then, closing the hatch behind us. With the dim light from outside cut off, it was completely dark inside. Plastic crinkled under my feet and I heard Loki digging in his pack.

"Just a second," he said. =

Then, a wan, warm light bloomed in the dark as Loki turned on his lantern. We were sitting on stacks of boxes, shrink wrapped in plastic and strapped to pallets. There was just enough space between the top of the stack and the roof of the container for us to crouch or sit upright.

Loki turned to me. "I feel one coming on," he said, lifting a trembling hand.

A moment later, his body went rigid, and he fell backward as I rushed to help.

CHAPTER II

Across the Border

L oki lay exhausted from his seizure, sprawled on one of the palleted and wrapped stacks of boxes. It had been over half an hour since we broke into the container. My active worry that we would be discovered had subsided into a general anxiety. I sat awkwardly next to Loki. His face was slack and his eyes jumped under the lids. Xel sat on his other side, monitoring his vital signs.

"He is sleeping soundly now. His brain activity has calmed," Xel said.

I nodded, still watching his face, his chest rising and falling. Somewhere far off, I heard a low droning sound. I ignored it at first but it steadily became louder and louder. Then suddenly—Crash!—a deafening noise and impact shook the entire container, knocking me sideways. The shaking was soon followed by a sickening sensation of movement.

"What's happening, Xel?" I yelled.

"A crane has picked up the container. They're putting us on a truck," he shouted back.

It felt like the whole container was being lifted high in the air then swung in an arc. I held on to Loki to keep him from sliding. We came to a stop, swinging back and forth for a moment, before the container began to lower slowly down.

Finally, there came a bump and a sound of metal hitting metal as the steel box made contact with the flatbed of a truck. More clanking and banging followed as various parts were folded and fitted to lock our box into place. I imagined robot arms fastening us onto the flatbed but it could have been real people. I just hoped nobody was going to check the hatches or open the doors. As a precaution, I reached over and turned off the lantern.

We sat there in the dark for another ten minutes until, with a jolt, we began to move. I imagined the truck passing between rows of other containers, stopping at the gate, turning onto the road we had crossed. For a while, the truck continued to move slowly. I could feel the powerful motor humming, gearing up and down. Eventually, after a couple of turns and an incline that might have been an onramp, we accelerated quickly. I could feel that we were moving fast and, before long, the truck settled into a steady pace, probably in a pack of other autotrucks, caravanning on the freeway.

My body began to relax. I had been holding myself tense for an hour or more. After a while, I realized it was still completely dark. I had been squeezing my eyes closed, imagining what was happening outside. I fumbled around until I found the lantern and turned it on low. Xel was there, on the other side of Loki still, gazing at me with his usual implacable expression. His shadow loomed huge on the wall of the container.

"Can you tell where we are, Xel?"

"No. I'm not getting any signal through this steel. Please open the hatch, and I will try again."

I crouched below the hatch and pushed it open. Luckily, it was mostly shielded from the wind by the tall engine cabin of the truck. Still it was almost wrenched out of my grip. The sky above was clear and full of stars.

"Yes. I'm getting signal now. We are on Interstate Five, heading north."

"Unbelievable," I answered. "We actually made it."

"We have not made it yet, but our chances have improved greatly," he said, gazing steadily at me.

I sat thinking for a while. It occurred to me that I had no idea how we would get out of the container and off the truck when the time came. "What happens now, Xel? How do we get out when we get to Oregon?"

"There is a weigh station north of Eugene. The auto-trucks do not actually come to a full stop but they do slow down considerably. We will have to jump off the truck there and walk back. We will have overshot by approximately ten miles, a full day of walking."

"How long until we get there?"

"We should be there in a little over eight hours. We seem to be traveling at almost exactly one hundred miles per hour, judging by my sampling of GPS readings."

"I guess I'll sleep for a while then," I said, yawning. "There's no chance we'll stop before then?"

"I don't think so. Not unless they suspect we have stowed away on this truck."

"All right," I said, spreading out my sleeping bag. "Wake me up if anything happens."

I lay back, resting my head on my arm, staring at the ceiling of the container. Wind was whipping in through the open hatch but the fresh air was nice so I left it open. I thought it might take me a while to calm down and fall asleep. I was exhausted though. All the activity of the day had worn me out. Almost immediately, I felt consciousness draining away into the dark as my eyelids fluttered closed.

శుసౌ

Loki woke me up, shaking my shoulder and saying my name. "Tara, wake up."

"What?" I asked, struggling out of sleep. "What time is it? Are we there? I'm starving," I said, sitting up.

"It's four a.m. We're about thirty miles from the weigh station. We need to start getting ready."

"Okay," I answered.

I dug a nutrient packet from my rucksack and added it to the last of the water in my bottle. I rubbed sleep from my eyes and sat drinking the shake until it was all gone. My body and mind were weary. But we were in PacNW cluster, I realized suddenly! We must have passed over the border while I was sleeping. We had made it—as long as we were able to get off the truck without killing ourselves.

"Were you awake when we crossed the border?" I asked Loki.

"No. I slept through it too. I just woke up half an hour ago. Xel told me about the weigh station. I guess these autotrucks don't ever really stop until they get to where they're going. We're really in old Oregon now though. It started to rain a while back and I had to close the hatch. When I put my head out there were trees everywhere and it smelled like pine and rain." Loki seemed energized, maybe even happy.

"I can smell it in the air," I said, agreeing.

He was right. Even with the hatch closed, I could feel the damp of the rain and the coolness. We crouched there, waiting, for the next twenty minutes.

Finally, Xel spoke. "It's time to get ready. The truck

will slow down when it is approaching the turn off. Once we pull off the freeway, we will continue to slow. We will roll over the weigh station scales at about five miles per hour then begin to speed up again to merge back onto the freeway. We need to jump off at the slowest speed. We will have about twenty seconds. Loki should be looking out the hatch. As soon as we begin to slow, he should climb out and crawl to the ladder. Tara, you follow him. I will come last. Climb to the bottom of the ladder and jump off. There will be another truck behind us so you will have to jump sideways and roll out of the way."

Loki and I glanced at each other then looked back at Xel.

"All right," Loki said. "I'm ready."

"Me too," I replied.

Loki pushed the hatch open and stood up, his head and shoulders sticking out the top. We had both put on our rain gear. His poncho whipped about in the wind. I crouched next to him, looking up. My heart was beating fast and my palms were itching. I closed my eyes for an instant, breathing deep. I thought I felt the truck begin to slow.

"Now," Loki called out and scrambled up through the hatch.

As soon as his feet were through, I followed. The rain and cold hit me immediately. I kept going, managing to get out and crawl along the top of the container, holding on to the steel struts and moving as fast as I could. The truck seemed to slow even more. I made it the edge and saw Loki below, hanging onto the rungs. Another truck was following us about fifteen meters back. Its headlights shone bright on Loki's wet poncho. I turned carefully and lowered my feet to the rung above where his hands were. The steel was cold and slippery and the wind was blowing rain in my face. I shook my head to get the water out of my eyes. There was a loud, dull thud as the truck crossed from asphalt roadway onto the massive steel plate that I supposed was the scale. I glanced down and saw Loki fling himself from the ladder. Quickly, I climbed down after him. My hand slipped off a rung, and I floundered for a moment but regained my grip. There was a bump as the rear wheels moved back onto asphalt. Now or never, I thought, and jumped. As I flew through the air, I marveled for a moment at how far I had jumped. My legs were definitely stronger now. A dark shape flew above me—Xel leaping from the top of the container. Then I hit the pavement, my knees buckled, and I rolled over and over, leaving the asphalt and finally coming to a stop in a patch of wet weeds and mud. I lay there dazed. My poncho had been caught by the wind and I could feel cold rain dripping on my side. Something hard in my backpack was poking me between my shoulder blades. After a time I felt something wet touch my face.

"Are you all right, Tara?" It was Xel.

I turned my head and saw his eyes. Loki was walking toward us. Another autotruck hit the scales with a loud bang and then accelerated away from us.

"Can you stand?" Loki asked. "We should get away from here."

"Yes," I answered, pushing up onto my elbows. I got my legs under me and stood shakily. "We made it," I said, looking from Loki to Xel. "We're in Oregon."

Loki was smiling back at me. Xel was nodding.

"Yeah," Loki said. "We made it. We need to get moving though."

Xel led us away from the brightly lit weigh station into a stand of tall trees. The freeway was nearby and I could hear trucks flashing by and see their lights. Rain dripped down from the branches above. I took a deep breath. The air smelled like home—full of aromas of grass and dirt and rotting leaves and pine needles. Beneath my feet the ground was soft.

"From here, we will need to get across the highway," Xel said. "We can wait at the tree line for an opening then run across. There is a wide median. We will run there then get down and wait for another opening to get across to the far side. There is a road close by that will take us west to the old highway Ninety-Nine. We can walk along Ninety-Nine South to Eugene."

A raindrop fell from my hood onto my nose when I nodded my agreement. Xel turned and we followed him.

The autotrucks were fast but they traveled in packs with plenty of space in between. Soon there was a break and we darted across to the median. Another break came and we ran to the far side, leapt over a ditch, and waded through tall grass and mud that pulled at my feet with every step. Finally, we came up an embankment and found a one lane gravel road.

"This is it," Xel said.

He turned west and led us away from the bright lights of the freeway, into the dark.

ↄ⃝ↄ⃝ↄ

Around mid-morning the rain stopped, and the sun came out in short bursts as a relentless wind from the west pushed patchy clouds across the sky. It was cold. I guess I had started to get used to the heat down south like my mom said I would. I put on every layer I had, but the wind still chilled my face. For Loki it was worse. He had lived in Los Angeles for his whole life, or as long as he could remember anyway. Luckily, we had brought high quality military surplus cold weather gear. Still, Loki was

worn out from his seizure the night before. He walked slowly and spoke little.

We had been traveling all day along train tracks that paralleled the highway. Overgrown fields spread out on both sides. Occasionally, we passed farmhouses that seemed occupied, with dogs and livestock and cultivated land, but most of the fields and farms were deserted. There were trestle bridges over clear streams where we struggled down through blackberry brambles to fill our water bottles, red tailed hawks high above, old train cars abandoned and rusting by the side of the tracks. Just after noon, we stopped for lunch, sitting in the open doorway of an old railcar. The sun was warm on my legs and I was sleepy. I looked over at Loki and saw that he was half asleep, his instafood meal forgotten in his lap.

"Let's stop here," I said. "We can camp in this railcar and walk the rest of the way tomorrow."

Xel was watching Loki too.

"No, I can keep going," Loki said, rousing himself. "Let's get to your grandmother's house."

I shook my head. "You're worn out. So am I. Another half a day doesn't matter. Let's stop here."

"Good idea," Xel said. "You should set up the tent inside the railcar in case it starts to rain again. The roof looks leaky."

I spent the rest of the afternoon wandering around but staying close to our camp while Loki slept. I found a small stream with trees growing on both banks, the branches arching over and forming a solid canopy overhead. It was colder in the shade by the water but I stayed there for a while, tossing leaves and sticks in and watching the current slowly carry them away. It reminded me of the stream behind our old house where I used to play. I missed that stream. Sitting there, gazing at the water, I realized it was one of the things I had missed the most after we moved and started living in the corp world. The TenCat housing, my school, the perfect sidewalks, and carefully tended landscaping—everything there was artificial. There was no nature, no room for anything random, no weeds, no fallen leaves. Nothing growing without human intervention. Water had always fascinated me. I used to spend hours by the stream behind our house. In the fall, red and gold leaves would drop from the trees, drift down onto the water, and then be carried slowly away. In winter, the edges would sometimes be icy. In spring and summer, the water striders would gather in the shallow, still parts, skipping across the surface. Somebody else was probably living in that house now. I thought about my old room but with someone else's things in it, the walls blank instead of covered with my posters and drawings, different curtains on the window. My vision blurred as tears welled up. I took a deep breath and calmed myself. I would probably never see that house again. I wouldn't be able to go back there.

We were running low on rations, but I made a full dinner. Loki looked like he needed it. We both ate every morsel. After we cleaned up, Loki played his flute for us, and I read from Aeon's book. Huddled around the fusion-battery-powered lantern light in our little tent, with wild, dark Oregon surrounding us, a feeling came over me. I wasn't sure at first what is was but after a while it dawned on me that it was happiness, or maybe even joy. We had only been companions for a few days, but I felt like we were becoming a sort of small family, protecting and caring for each other, bonded by our journey and the things we had been through. It wasn't like anything I had felt before. My own family had always been sort of weird and awkward. I suppose my parents loved me but they never said so. My sister was a brat and treated me and our parents like hopeless freaks. She was the only normal one. The psychologists would call her prosocial, properly oriented I guess. I had often felt judged—for being weird, for not always being able to control my emotions, for not being good at making friends—not just by strangers and classmates, but by my own family. Now, though, with Xel and Loki, it felt like a kind of trust and quiet acceptance of each other had grown between us. Xel, although artificial, felt like a full member of our family. I realized with a shock that I had begun to think of him as a someone instead of a something. Whatever I had done to his programming, it had released a humanity in him that he hadn't possessed before. I glanced at their faces while I read. They were both listening intently, wrapped up in the story. I realized that I loved both of them. Quiet, scarred, strong Loki and capable, rational, protective Xel. They were like brothers I thought, not knowing for sure what it was like to have a brother but thinking it might be like having Xel and Loki. Ever since the night I spent on the roof of the hospital, I had been more and more aware of a kind of knotted, compressed, tightly bound clump of shame and humiliation at the center of my being. I felt in some ways like part of me was a small child, huddled up, unable to speak what I felt, pushing everything back in upon itself, locking my true self away so that nobody would see me or notice me. Something had started to untangle over the days I had spent on the run though. A crack had opened, a knot had come undone, some of the tension had released. And I felt happy.

ℰᴖℰᴖ

The next day, we passed through a couple of small towns. The railroad tracks ran through the outskirts so we kept to them and avoided the busier main street areas. Xel stayed hidden, following us but staying in the grass or among the trees. We did see a few people. There were a couple of kids in a big yard, digging with sticks, who watched us silently as we passed. An old man sitting in a truck parked on an access road tipped his hat to us and nodded.

"Was that a self-operated car?" Loki asked, amazed.

"Yes. I think so," I answered. "Although most old cars here are retrofitted with operating computers."

We saw more old cars and newer autocars passing by overhead when we crossed under overpasses. Once, a passenger train came down the tracks heading south. We crouched in the weeds and watched it go by, hands over our ears. All in all, the people we saw didn't pay us much attention. It wasn't unusual in PacNW to see people on the move, wandering from place to place looking for work. People were poor. If anyone saw how young we were, they might have asked questions but, from a distance, we were unremarkable.

We finally reached Eugene around one p.m. I was tired but feeling excited. I couldn't wait to see my grandmother. I was sure she would be able to help us. Her house was near the tracks, in an area of town called Whitacre so we stayed walking along the tracks all the way into town. I had never come from that direction so it took me a little while to orient myself, but with Xel's help, I found the right place to turn off from the railway and begin heading in toward the neighborhoods. It was an area of low warehouses, cinder block buildings, and giant empty lots full of weeds. As we moved farther from the tracks though, we began to see small, single family houses. It had begun to rain again—tiny drops drizzling down out of leaden clouds. We slouched up Blair Street, passed a small business area with a little grocery store and a tea house, then turned down Fourth. I walked ahead, speeding up. Emotions were coming fast and making my stomach hurt, my head swim. We were half a block away. *I hope she's home*, I thought, willing her to be there. It was a Saturday. She was usually home on weekends. At last, I stood in front of her house. It was a small, tidy house, painted gray. There were three steps up to a front porch, then the door. I didn't see any lights in the windows. I glanced to the right and saw Loki and Xel, half a block away, hanging back. Resolutely, then, I walked up the path, climbed the steps to the porch, and knocked on the door. While I waited I looked at the old wicker rocking chair to the right of the door. It was covered with a big red and orange piece of cloth. There was a patch of fur on the seat where my grandmother's cat Alexi liked to sit. No answer came. I knocked again and called out this time.

"Grandma? It's Tara." Still no answer came. I heard a sound and turned toward it.

The front door of the neighbor's house was open and I saw Mrs. Sullivan looking around the jamb.

She saw me and waved. "Tara! Are you looking for your grandma?"

"Yes," I called back.

"She's not here. She went up north. Called up to help with the flu epidemic in Portland. She won't be back for a month or more. It's all quarantined up there. Only medical personnel in and out. I'm taking care of Alexi for her."

I felt my stomach sinking and a hollow, numb, blackness growing inside me. My ears were buzzing. How could she be gone? For a month or more? I needed her. I shook my head, forced myself to call back. "Thanks."

I realized I should say something else, but I couldn't think of anything. Instead I turned and began walking back toward Loki.

"Tara, what are you doing here anyway? I thought you all moved down south," she called after me but I didn't turn. I just kept walking, straight past Loki. Half a block later I found a bus stop and sat down on the bench. I rested my head in my hands. I was rocking back and forth. Hot tears came, and I began to cry. I heard a low keening moan and realized after a moment that it was coming from me. I couldn't stop. It was all too much—to find her gone after making it, against all odds, to Eugene! I felt Xel leaning his head on my shoulder. On my other side, Loki sat next to me. He took my hand and held it. I knew I needed to pull myself together. I took a deep rattling breath, then another, turned and looked at Xel then Loki.

"She's not here," I said. "She's away helping with a flu epidemic. Maybe for a month or more. What are we going to do now?"

CHAPTER 12

Running Again

We had been sitting at the bus stop for several minutes, each silently thinking our own thoughts while the rain drizzled down around us. I was feeling defeated and helpless. The emotion wrapped me up like dark wings. All of the calm and happiness I had felt the night before seemed dashed away—replaced by confusion. I couldn't imagine what we were going to do. I watched the raindrops rippling a puddle, my mind unfocused. I felt out of control, like my brain was spinning off into space. I was losing my grip. Fiercely, I began reciting to myself the titles of old science fiction books I had read, starting with an author, then going over every book title I could remember, then moving on to another author.

I got stuck, trying to remember the name of a book, and felt myself beginning to unravel again. I doubled down, and the title came to me. Slowly, the exercise brought me back under control. It was something I had started doing when I was younger and learning to deal with my meltdowns. It had been a while but I found it still worked. Finally, a thought came to me, unfolding slowly like a flower opening. At first it was just a feeling—a tiny blossoming of hope. Then it solidified into an image: Rosie. We could go to Rosie's house! It wasn't far. We could ask her mother for help. I laughed when I thought of it. Loki and Xel both looked at me, waiting for me to tell them what was funny.

"We can go to my friend Rosie's house," I said. "Her mom is cool. She'll help us."

"Are you sure?" Xel asked. "We don't want to contact anyone who will turn us in. The police here will send us back if they find out who we are. They don't want trouble with the federalist clusters."

"I think so," I said. "Rosie is my best friend."

"Maybe you should go by yourself then. Loki and I can wait nearby. Make sure she is okay with you bringing us to her house. Come get us if everything seems all right."

Loki and I agreed that Xel's plan was sensible. Rosie's house was close—only a mile away. Soon we were walking through another old residential area where giant trees lifted the sidewalk with their roots and the roofs of the houses were covered with moss. Rain dripped steadily down but it wasn't a downpour and our ponchos kept us dry. Xel's artificial fur shed the water without ever looking wet. There was a narrow alley that passed by Rosie's back yard. I decided to lead them that way and leave them in the alley while I went in. There was a garage facing onto the alley with a roof that extended out a few feet. They huddled in the dry area under the overhang. Loki leaned against the garage door, hands in his pockets, shoulders hunched against the cold.

"I'll be back soon," I said.

They both nodded. Loki looked wary.

"Be careful," he said.

"I will," I answered and turned to the gate that let into the back yard.

As soon as I closed the gate behind me, I heard a bark and a giant, fluffy black dog came bounding around the side of the house.

"Rufus," I called and he ran to me through the wet grass, yelping. I hugged him while he licked my face. "It's good to see you. Is Rosie home?"

"Who's back here?" The screen door at the rear of the house banged open, and I saw Rosie's mom, Wen, standing in the doorway.

"Wen, it's me, Tara." I stood, my hand buried in Rufus's fur.

Wen's face was confused for a moment. She stared hard at me across the yard and tapped her specs, issuing a softly spoken command to zoom in on my face.

Then she smiled. "Tara! What are you doing here? Come give me a hug. Are you back for a visit?"

"Sort of," I answered. Walking across to meet her. "I'll tell you all about it. Is Rosie home?"

"No, she's at her dad's house on the coast. She'll be back tomorrow night."

A strong feeling of disappointment surged up in my chest but it was better, actually. I needed to talk to Wen alone.

I reached the door and she hugged me. "Come in out of the rain. You grew!"

Half an hour later, we were sitting at her kitchen table with cold cups of tea. I had told her everything in my halting, back and forth way.

"This is really serious, Tara. I need to think. You can stay here tonight, and we'll talk about next steps tomorrow. And your friends too. Where are they? Out back? Go invite them in."

"Thanks," I said, overwhelmed, hugging Wen again. "I'll go get them."

Soon we were all back inside the little house, and I was introducing Loki and Xel. Wen was fascinated by Xel. She was an AI researcher at the university. Rufus, though, wasn't so sure about Xel. He kept whining and whimpering and looking at Wen for permission to attack the furry intruder. Finally, Wen put him outside where he sat on the back stoop with his head on his paws. Loki and I took showers for the first time in days. It felt like heaven to be under the warm water. Wen found warm robes for both of us then put our traveling clothes in her rattley old washer. As evening fell, we cooked a simple meal of beans, rice, onions, and bell peppers from the garden, and homemade tortillas. Loki helped cook, and Wen seemed surprised by his skill. I explained to her how they lived at the garage, and he told her about the community gardens. I was a hopeless cook so I sat back and just enjoyed the warm kitchen, the good smells, and the rain falling outside. The old oak table and the white tiles yellowed with age were comfortingly familiar. It was almost like being back in my old house.

When dinner was done and the dishes were washed and put away, first Loki, then I, began to yawn uncontrollably.

"I think you two need to go to bed," Wen said, looking from me to Loki.

"I think you're right," I answered around another yawn.

The house had only two bedrooms. Wen gave me Rosie's room and made up the couch for Loki.

"I don't suppose you sleep," she said, looking at Xel.

"No, but I will stay with Tara," he answered.

I thanked Wen again for letting us stay, said goodnight to Loki, and went to Rosie's room. Xel hopped up next to me where I sat on the bed. It felt weird to be there by myself. Everything was weird lately though so I shrugged it off. Snuggled down under two layers of blankets and a quilt, I reached over and turned off the light. I hadn't slept in a bed since the night before I ran away. My body seemed to melt into the mattress. Xel was curled at my feet.

"Goodnight, Tara."

"Goodnight, Xel," I whispered. "Do you think we can trust Wen?"

"I don't know," he answered. "I hope so."

"Me too," I said, laying my head down on the pillow.

☙❧☙

I woke in darkness to Xel pawing my shoulder. "Tara. Wake up. We have to go."

"What is it?" I asked, instantly awake.

"Wen is on a voice chat with someone from TenCat Corp. I am sorry to admit that I did not trust her. I have been monitoring the traffic on the local network in this house."

"TenCat?"

"Yes. She has informed them that we are here."

"Crap." Immediately my heart began to race and adrenaline kicked in. I tossed Rosie's quilt aside and fumbled in the dark for my clothes. Luckily my clean laundry was put away neatly in my backpack. I had become very strict about packing my things and keeping them in order since I'd started living out of a backpack. It was one of the ways I dealt with the chaos of our journey.

"We should wake up Loki," I said, pulling on my padded vest.

"I already did. He's getting ready."

In the living room, I found Loki dressed, with his pack already on. He was agitated, pacing back and forth.

"Let's go," I said.

Loki nodded but then stopped in his tracks, looking toward the doorway that led from the living room to the kitchen. Wen was standing there, her face frozen. She was wearing her specs. I faced her, not knowing what to say, my head still muddled from being woken so abruptly.

"I'm sorry," she said finally, her voice breaking. "They contacted me. They said you might come here. They threatened to take Rosie away. They said I had to tell them if you came here—"

"I'm sorry, too," I answered haltingly. "We shouldn't have come. We put you in a bad position."

"You have until morning. They said they would contact the police. They'll come for you in the morning. I'll tell them I fell asleep. I didn't hear you leave. Run. Get as far away as you can before then."

Out on the sidewalk, it was cold and very dark but at least the rain had stopped. Gusts of wind battered me as I led Xel and Loki back the way we had come, toward the railroad tracks. It was the only thing I could think of. We could get away from town, hopefully hop a freight train. We went as fast as possible, running across the street at lighted intersections, walking fast. As we approached Seventh Street though, Xel called to me.

"Tara, stop."

I turned. Loki was standing, unmoving. I could barely see his face in the darkness.

"Loki! Are you all right?"

He didn't answer. I walked back and put a hand on his arm. He was trembling. He opened his mouth to speak but the words froze, unspoken, as his body stiffened. His eyes locked on mine, and he stood absolutely still for a

moment then abruptly slumped and crumpled toward the ground. I caught him as he fell, getting my arms around his chest. Crouched down on the sidewalk with his weight on my legs, I looked to Xel helplessly.

"What are we going to do?" I cried in frustration.

"Drag him that way, into the carport."

I followed Xel's gaze and saw that we were in the driveway of a small house. At the end was a dark carport with what appeared to be a car parked in it. It was covered with a tarp but was definitely automobile-shaped. I straightened my legs and dragged Loki up the driveway. His heels bumped along the ground and through piles of wet leaves. He was still convulsing. When we were under the roof of the carport, we stopped, and I laid him down on the concrete floor.

"Try the car door. See if it's open," Xel said.

I lifted the canvas. The car had old fashioned door handles. It was a four door. It took me a minute to figure out that I needed to push the button in to disengage the latch then pull to open the door. I tried the rear door on the driver side and it creaked open with a screech of old hinges. Inside I saw a wide stretch of back seat in the dim light from a streetlight half a block away.

"Get him inside. You'll have to lift him," Xel advised.

I took Loki's pack off his back, tossed it into the car, then squatted, and lifted him again. It was awkward, but I managed to get him in by essentially falling backward, landing in the backseat with his body on top of me, then squirming out from under him and crawling over him to get out. I pushed him the rest of the way in, turned him on his side with his knees bent, then got back in, and sat next to him. I dug the lantern out of his pack and set it on the floor turned to its lowest setting, then managed to pull the edge of the tarp back down and close the door. Xel had hopped into the car and was sitting in the front passenger seat. We were hidden for the time being. The interior smelled musty, like mildew and motor oil. Loki lay still now, his seizure over but still unconscious. I put a hand on his back, feeling his breathing.

"What now, Xel? He won't be able to travel for a while."

"Just a moment. This vehicle has been retrofitted with an onboard computer and fusion drive to replace the original internal combustion engine. I am attempting to interface. The communication protocol is very old. I am searching for a proper network stack. Yes. Found it. Installing. Good. It requests authentication. Give me a moment. The cryptographic scheme is out of date. It was broken years ago. Working. Working. I have defeated it. Now, this is not a modern operating computer. It can't drive the car in full automatic mode. It only assists when it recognizes danger. It also collects data and performs basic functions. You will have to drive, Tara."

"*What*?"

"You will have to operate the car."

"I don't know how!"

"It is our best hope. You will have to try. I will assist you with instructions. If we do not get as far away from here as possible in the time we have, they will surely find us and send us back. I will be factory reset. You will have the device implanted. We can only guess what will happen to Loki."

I crawled into the front and sat in the driver's seat, gripping the steering wheel with both hands, staring straight ahead. I was terrified and at the end of my patience. It was unfair. Why was it me who had to run? Why was I singled out and pushed from place to place with no control over my own life? It felt like I was just reacting, like a bug that ran when you turned on a light. I could feel my face flushing. A wild anger was burning in me. I knew Xel was right, though. We had to get away. I was gripping the steering wheel so hard my knuckles were white.

"Okay. I'll try," I said through gritted teeth. "What do I need to do?"

"First, remove the tarp."

"What if the people in the house wake up?"

"We must be very quiet. I have just pulled a diagram of this house from the city property database. The bedrooms appear to be in the rear."

The tarp was heavy but I managed to drag it off. When I was back inside and seated in the driver seat, Xel commanded the computer to power up the car. It came to life with a low hum, lights glowing on the dashboard.

"What kind of car is this?" I asked.

"Volvo One-Sixty-Four-e," he replied. "Built in 1975. Step on the left pedal with your right foot then move the lever there to R."

The car bucked and lurched as I backed it slowly down the driveway, pumping the brake pedal every time it felt out of control. I turned the wheel too far and almost took out a shrub as I made the backward turn onto the street. Luckily, there were no other cars on the road. It was the middle of the night. Xel gave directions and I followed them, driving haltingly through the tree-lined, residential streets. The car felt incredibly heavy—like a giant rolling brick. I slowly became more accustomed to the steering, learning how far I needed to turn the wheel. I was still stepping too hard on the brake pedal though, making the car lurch with every stop. Driving was stressful but also thrilling in a dangerous kind of way. It took every bit of concentration I had. If we hadn't been on the run from the police, with Loki in the back, his face slack and drained looking in the light from the streetlamps, if it had been different circumstances—thirty years ago and me just learning to drive for the first time—it might have been kind of fun.

Soon we came to the downtown area of Eugene, and we had to move onto larger streets with some occasional traffic. The other cars were all autocabs though. They were programmed to keep a safe distance. One of them passed us in the left lane, and I caught a brief glimpse of a man's face, peering at us curiously out the rear window.

Following Xel's directions, I drove along Franklin Boulevard with the big buildings and lights of the university on our right, crossed a bridge over the dark, swift water of the Willamette River, then passed through a derelict area that had once been downtown Springfield. Before long, we were outside of the populated areas, traveling along Highway 126 in the dark. I was going slow but even so, the trees seemed to blur on either side, rushing past. Every so often, we would pass an old building or house. There were no lights though. Just the headlamps of our car, illuminating the road ahead. My tension eased a bit.

"We made it out of the city," I said.

"Yes," Xel answered, hopping into the passenger seat from the back. "Loki is sleeping but his brain activity is still abnormal. I'm afraid this seizure is worse than the others we have seen."

"What are we going to do? We need to get him help."

"I don't know. I thought this would be the best direction to go. They will assume we are heading north, toward the quarantine zone, to find your grandmother. Or back south. Probably not east. We will have to abandon this vehicle soon. They will search for us by floater when they find we have run again."

"We'll drive until early morning then. We'll have to

hide the car somewhere while it's still dark then camp nearby. We need to make sure somebody will find the car though. It seems like the owner put a lot of work into restoring it. I feel bad about stealing it."

"Yes. We can find a way. I also feel bad about it. We had very little choice, though."

"I can't believe I was so stupid, Xel. Why did we go to Wen? I should have thought of the possibility that they might contact her. If my grandmother was home, it would have been even worse. They would have found a way to force her to turn against us too."

"Perhaps."

"Thanks for hacking her network and warning us." I shuddered, thinking about what would have happened.

"Of course."

"I've been thinking, Xel. It came to me the night before last actually—something I forgot with all the chaos. The day before my mom took me to the psychiatrist, I got a weird message. It was just some GPS coordinates. It said something like 'freedom and safety' then just had the coordinates, and it came from an anonymous account. Then I got another one right after I decided to run, but I didn't read it. Looking back now, it almost seems like somebody was trying to warn me. Maybe they were offering help."

"Interesting," Xel responded. "I would be suspicious of a strange message from an anonymous source. May I access your specs and look at it?"

"Sure. They're in the side pocket of my pack. The messages were downloaded so you should be able to find them. I need to leave the data connection off in case they can track me that way."

Xel jumped into the back of the car. A minute later, he jumped back into the front with the case in his mouth. It was scary to take a hand off the wheel but I quickly reached over, opened the case, pressed the contact to power them up, and put them on. They would not work unless I was wearing them since they were locked to my biometrics. I saw an alert asking to allow access and quickly gave the okay. After that, I put them in audio only mode. It was hard enough to drive the car without distractions.

"The messages are interesting," Xel said after a while. "The sender has skillfully hidden himself by passing the data through proxies and hacked servers. I cannot determine where they came from. The coordinates given are approximately seventy miles northeast from here. This is odd since the message was sent before we decided to come here."

"Yeah, weird. What does the second one say?"

"It lists the same coordinates and simply says 'Find your way to us. We can help.'"

"What do you think?"

"It seems more than coincidental that you received these messages exactly when you needed help and a place to go. It's as if somebody, somewhere, knew what was happening and reached out. However, it could also be a trap set for you by the TenCat doctors anticipating that you might run. Why would they direct you to the Pacific Northwest cluster though? If they thought you might run away, they would give you coordinates close by. Somewhere easier and quicker. It does not seem logical that they would do this at all, though. They did not have any reason to think that you would be suspicious."

"Could it be my grandmother? Maybe she knew. Maybe my mom or dad talked to her about it."

"Possible."

"I have a feeling about this, Xel. I want to go there, to the coordinates. We'll have to ditch the car and go on

foot. We can scope it out. If it seems like a trap, we can turn around."

"Let's discuss it with Loki when he is awake."

"Okay. Does this work?" I asked, reaching out and turning a knob on the dashboard. The old fashioned radio lit up and a low sound of static filled the car. "How do you operate it?"

"Turn the knob on the right to adjust the frequency. I doubt we will find any stations though. The commercial radio stations died out years ago."

Keeping my eyes on the road, I turned the knob all the way to the left then slowly moved the pointer across the dial. It was almost at the end when the static broke up and a tinny, twangy sound of guitar notes replaced it. A woman was singing. At first, the words were mixed with patches of static, and I couldn't understand them, but then the sound cleared up for a moment and I heard her sing:

"I raised my head and set myself
In the eye of the storm, in the belly of a whale.
My spirit stood on solid ground.
I'll be at peace when they lay me down"

The words and the way she sang them struck me. I felt like I was in the eye of the storm, out on that road, restlessly wandering, buffeted, and pushed from one place to another.

"I wonder who is broadcasting out here. It must be a hobbyist," Xel mused.

"I don't know," I said. "I like the music though."

I left the dial there and the music continued through bursts of static—a lonesome melody reaching out across the night as we drove deeper into the wilderness of old Oregon.

CHAPTER 13

The Homestead

Near daybreak, Xel spotted an old garage just off the highway. I slowed, turned the car around, and drove back to it. The road had become more and more uneven throughout the night with patches buckled by tree roots and big pot holes, with branches and other debris scattered across the surface. Several times, I had seen the eyes of nocturnal animals glowing in the head-lights. At the end, I was driving a mere five or ten miles per hour. Getting much farther by car would have been impossible anyway.

Following Xel's instructions, I stopped, moved the lever to park, and set the break. Even in the twilight of early morning, I could see that the garage was not in great shape. It had space for two cars but the roof had fallen in on one side. The side that still had a roof had no door, just a gaping frame beyond which was a cement floor scattered with leaves. There was a jumble of old machin-ery and broken furniture at the back, but it looked big enough to house the car. I got back in and carefully pulled forward until the front of the car bumped up against the pile of junk. I got out then and checked the back. It was all the way inside—hidden from above. Still, I decided it would be better to hide it as completely as possible. Rummaging through the junk pile, I found an old sheet of plastic, yellowed and stained with paint drips. I covered the back of the car with the drop cloth then piled as much other junk as I could move around the car to camouflage it more.

I was exhausted. My eyes felt gritty and my body ached with lack of sleep. I still needed to set up camp and somehow get Loki out of the car and inside our tent. Xel came back from scoping out the area and told me there was a copse of big fir trees nearby, down a slope from the road and dense enough to hide us from floaters above.

I followed him there with the two packs and set up the tent. It was about a hundred yards from the garage. I went back, shivering in the early morning damp, and opened the rear car door. Loki was still passed out, breathing slowly. I sat him up and managed to turn him around. He felt solid but not so heavy as before. He hadn't lost weight—I had grown stronger. I put my arms around his chest and pulled him as gently as possible out of the car. His head rested on my chest as I dragged him, step by staggering step, all the way to the copse and into the tent. By the time I laid him down, the muscles in my arms were burning with the exertion. I flopped down on my own sleeping bag.

Xel sat in the entrance to the tent. "You should try to get some water in him. Sit him up and drip it into his mouth."

I did as he suggested. Loki stirred, eyes moving under the lids but not opening. He muttered something when I lowered him back down. I zipped the tent closed and turned on the heater built into the lantern to keep him warm.

"My sensors still show abnormal brain activity. Small spikes followed by slow delta waves. I will keep watch. You should sleep."

"Yeah," I replied, rubbing my eyes and yawning. "I'm pretty tired."

ⅇ⁄ᴐⅇ⁄ᴐ

It was past noon when I woke up. Loki was still sleeping next to me and the lantern was pumping out warmth. I stretched and sat up. Dappled sunlight danced on the roof of the tent as a breeze moved the branches above. The tent door was partially unzipped. I poked my head out, looking around for Xel, but didn't see him. My stomach was growling with hunger. I dug through both packs, but we were out of rations. There was just one small packet of dried fruit and nuts left. I decided to wait to eat it until Loki woke up. He seemed calmer. I shook him gently but he wouldn't wake. It seemed to make him agitated so I stopped. I was worried. He had always slept after a seizure but he hadn't stayed asleep for so long. I stuck my head out again and saw Xel prowling through the trees, approaching the tent.

"There is an inhabited dwelling nearby," he said, stopping a few feet from the tent. "There are goats and chickens. I saw a small child and a woman. The house is well kept. We should avoid them and move on from here as soon as possible."

"Loki still hasn't woken, though. I'm worried about him, Xel. We can't go anywhere until he wakes up and can walk."

"Yes. I'm worried too."

"Also, we're out of food."

"I saw several species of edible mushrooms. There is chickweed, and goosefoot—both edible greens. I can show you where they are. Also, we are close to a river. The Mackenzie. There is a shallow area nearby where you could fish. There is a kit with hooks and fishing line in Loki's pack."

"I guess we'd better go gather what we can."

We left Loki sleeping in the tent, and I followed Xel into the woods. Xel looked at home among the trees and undergrowth, springing from root to rock to fallen log, paws soft and noiseless on the forest floor. He showed me the mushrooms and plants, but we decided to harvest them on the way back from the river. It wasn't far. We had to bushwhack down to the bank, my feet sinking deep into the layer of decaying pine needles and dead leaves that blanketed the ground. When we reached the river's edge, we found a broad shallows with a swift current flowing in the middle. There were several large boulders in the water near the bank. I stepped carefully on smaller stones and made my way to a mossy boulder that looked comfortable enough to spend some time sitting on. I had a good stick and, in an old tin can I found by the road, a couple of worms dug out of the forest floor. I hadn't ever fished before but Xel gave me instructions and soon I had the line in the water with a worm on the hook and was gently moving it back and forth, hoping for a bite.

I sat there for about fifteen minutes, moving the line, pulling it in, casting it back out. Finally, I felt something yank at the line. Then another yank.

"Pull it in slowly," Xel advised.

I took the fishing line in my hands and slowly gathered it in. I could tell there was no fish on the end though, even before the wormless hook emerged from the shining river.

"Fish ate the worm but didn't get hooked," I said, holding up the hook.

"We have some smart fish around here."

I jumped at the deep, male voice, and almost fell off the boulder. Whirling around, I saw a man standing about fifteen feet away, hand on a sapling growing near the river bank. He was dressed in old jeans and a flannel shirt. He looked middle-aged—maybe about my parents' age. His hair was long, tied back, speckled with gray. "They don't get caught easy. Probably not with a stick and ten feet of fishing line anyway. Best time is early morning. You might have a chance then."

Xel was hunkered down in front of me, ready to spring. He growled low and threatening.

"Whoa," the man said, holding up both hands. "I don't mean any harm. Not every day I see a girl with a tame bobcat fishing in my river. We don't see much of anyone around here to tell the truth. I just wanted to say hello."

"Who are you?" Xel asked.

The man's jaw dropped, and he stared for several seconds before responding. "Talking bobcat? You must be AI—robot cat."

"Yes, with very sharp claws," Xel answered.

The man held up his hands again. "Not looking for any trouble," he said. "That friend of yours back at your camp needs some help, though. I took a look in your tent. Thought nobody was home. My wife is an herbal healer. She can help him maybe."

My heart jumped in my chest. Quickly, though, I controlled myself, taking a deep breath. "We can't. We're just passing through."

"Don't worry about me," the man answered, as if reading my thoughts. "I'm not one to report anyone to the authorities. I don't have much to do with any govern-

ments or police. My name's Jed. My house is just down the river. Come knock on the door if you change your mind. I'll ask my wife to make some extra dinner tonight just in case." He backed away, turning, and walked off without a backward look.

I watched him go, my head full of emotions I couldn't untangle. "Let's go back, Xel. We're not going to catch any fish this way."

We gathered mushrooms and greens on the way back. It wouldn't be much, but I could make a soup maybe. When I crawled back into the tent, though, I saw immediately that Loki was worse. His face was tense and his body twitched randomly. His previously deep breathing was shallow, and he gasped every few breaths.

"Xel," I called, anxious. "He's not getting better. We need to do something."

Xel padded into the tent and observed Loki for a moment. "I agree. What was your opinion of the man by the river?" he asked.

I thought for a minute about our encounters with others since running away—the security guard who let me go, the shopkeeper at the surplus store, Aeon and Loki, the people in the sewer, Wen. It was a gamble every time. Still, I was glad I had decided to trust Aeon and Loki. The man had seemed simple and honest, like Aeon.

"He seemed honest," I said.

"Yes. I will go to his house. We need help. We do not have another choice. If his wife is really a doctor, she might be able to help."

"Okay," I said. "Ask him to come here. I can't carry Loki that whole way by myself."

Fifteen minutes later, Xel was back with the man, Jed. He looked in at Loki and shook his head once, sharply. "We need to get him back to the house. I'll carry him.

Leave your tent here for now. Bring your packs if you want."

He stooped, picked Loki up, and maneuvered him out of the tent. Once outside, he shifted Loki onto his shoulders in a fireman's carry. I followed, carrying both packs, and Xel trotted along with us. Loki's eyes didn't open but he seemed to stir a bit when Jed stepped over logs or hopped a patch of mud.

The house was in a clearing, with the river behind, down a steep, rocky slope at the back. Made of hewn logs stacked on top of each other, the house had a high, peaked roof shingled in some wood with a reddish tinge. There was a fenced paddock to one side where goats stood scattered about, giving us sidelong glances. On the other side was a chicken coop with several hens scratching in the dirt nearby. A big dog came loping around the house, barking, but Jed silenced it with a sharp command then carried Loki straight through the open front door. I followed him into an entry hall with a dark stone floor. Muddy boots were piled next to the door and jackets were hung on pegs.

"Del," he called. "This boy needs your help."

A woman ran into the hall, wiping strong hands on an apron. She looked at Loki, glanced at me and Xel with a searching expression, then turned back to Loki. She was similar in age to Jed, with black hair braided down her back. She wore a long dress of coarsely woven fabric beneath her apron. "Take him into Marigold's room. Lay him on the bed." she said.

Jed turned down a hallway that opened onto the entry hall. The woman followed and so did I. At the first door we came to, Jed turned again and laid Loki down on a little bed in the corner. It was a small, tidy room with a chest at the foot of the bed, a circular rug covering a wood-plank floor, and a window over the bed that let in enough light for the woman to examine Loki. She stooped over him while Jed, Xel, and I stood back by the door.

"Give her a minute," Jed whispered to me. "She'll know what to do."

While he spoke, the woman picked up Loki's hand and felt his pulse, put an ear to his chest, and lay her hands on his forehead and throat. For a little while, she stood, eyes closed, with her hand hovering in the air above his chest. Finally, she turned to us. "His condition is serious. He needs medicine. Valerian, skullcap. I'll make a tea."

She strode out of the room. I went to the bed, sat next to Loki, and took his hand in mine. Xel hopped up next to me.

"She will heal him," Jed said. "Don't worry."

I turned to him. "Thank you," I answered. "I don't know what we'd do—I'm Tara, by the way. This is Xel. And this is Loki."

Jed nodded. "Loki, is it? He's going to be okay. Don't you worry."

ᘒᘒᘒ

After sundown, I sat at the candlelit dinner table with Jed and his family. Their house had one big, high-ceilinged room with the kitchen, dining table, and sitting area all contained within it. A warm fire burned in a massive hearth made of river rock. Jed's wife was named Delia. They had two daughters, a two-year-old, Luna, and a four-year-old, Marigold. The girls stared at me with wide eyes, not speaking. Xel sat across the room, on a chair, gazing out the window. They stared at him too, alternating between us. Marigold had approached him earlier and run a hand over his head, but she had jumped back and hid behind her mother's skirts when he spoke to her. They seemed unused to company, and I was not good at speaking to them. I didn't have much experience with children other than my sister.

Earlier, Delia had dribbled the tea into Loki's mouth while I held him propped up. Within a few minutes, his body had calmed. Xel reported that his brain activity also became better, reverting to a normal sleep pattern. I sat with him, holding his hand, until Jed came and called me to dinner. I had asked Jed to give Delia the bag of mushrooms and greens I gathered and I found that she had incorporated them into the meal. It was a kind of pie with a vegetable, mushroom, and meat-filled crust. Jed told me the meat was venison. We ate in uncomfortable silence for a few minutes. I glanced up now and then to see Jed and Delia both looking my way and exchanging silent looks of their own.

Finally, Delia broke the silence. "Tara, is it?"

"Yes," I answered. "The food is delicious. Thanks for sharing it with me—and for helping Loki."

"You're welcome. We're always happy to help where we can. But I'm worried about you and your friend. What are you two doing wandering off by yourselves? The boy is sick. He needs more help than I can give."

"I know. He couldn't get help where we were. We came up here. My grandmother is a doctor. We were on our way to get help from her but she's gone, up in the north helping with an outbreak—" I broke off.

"She lives up here? By us?" Jed asked.

"No. In Eugene. We came up this way after we found out she was gone."

"Where are you headed?"

I glanced back and saw Xel looking at me, then I cast my eyes down while I thought about how to answer Jed's question. "We're headed up into the mountains to meet up with some other family members," I said finally. My lie did not sound convincing even to me.

Jed, Delia, and the two girls were all looking at me.

"Well," Delia said, "You're not going anywhere until your friend gets some rest. He'll need time to recover. You can stay with us, meanwhile."

"Thank you," I said again, staring at my plate.

ↄↄↄↄ

We ended up staying with them for three days. Loki woke up the morning after we arrived but he was weak and groggy. Delia ordered him to stay in bed and brought him food on trays. I found opportunities to speak with him alone, though and, with help from Xel, filled him in on where we were and what had happened.

I tried to make myself useful, helping Delia with housework and cooking and Marigold with her chores which included feeding the animals. Before long, Marigold decided I was all right and began chattering away at me, explaining how to feed the goats, gather firewood, and check for eggs in the chicken coop. She seemed happy to have somebody to boss around other than her little sister. Xel stayed with Loki mostly, watching him and monitoring the electrical activity in his brain. Jed spent most of the day outdoors, working on the house, which he had built himself, chopping wood, and gathering food. He came back in the evenings with fish, mushrooms, and other kinds of game and edibles.

On the second day, Delia and I were in the kitchen. She was kneading bread dough, and I was chopping onions.

"Why do you live out here?" I asked. "You don't even have a fusion cell."

"We're Thoreauvians," she answered without turning.

"What's that?" I replied.

"We follow the teachings of Henry David Thoreau. Haven't you heard of us? I guess not. Our movement started last century, back in the nineteen-sixties. A lot of people in this area moved out of the cities and took up a simpler life in the country when the plagues came."

"I see. So you don't ever go into town?"

"Twice a year. We make things and sell them at the markets, then use the money to buy supplies like flour, corn, sugar. We know other families who live in this area. Some have vehicles."

I liked Delia and Jed and their beautiful daughters. Their life was simple. They had no specs, no computers, not even electricity, but they didn't seem to miss those things. The girls didn't even know what a computer was. Their toys were stones, sticks, pieces of wood carved by Jed, paper and pencils, dolls hand sewn from scraps of fabric. After three days, though, I was anxious to get moving again.

On the morning of the fourth day, we ate breakfast with them and then prepared to go, standing in the entry hall. On an impulse, I dug the plasma knife out of my pack and offered it to Jed. He looked at it and shook his head.

"You keep that," he said. "You might need it on the road."

"What about this?" I asked, holding up my LED flashlight, "Can I give it to Marigold?"

Jed nodded his assent, and I crouched down, holding it out to the girl. She took it, and I showed her how to use it. Immediately, Luna tottered forward to see what it was.

"Thanks again for everything," I said, standing.

"From me too," Loki added. "Thanks for bringing me back. I was way out there. You saved my life," he continued, looking at his feet, embarrassed.

"We help who we can," Delia answered. "Sometimes others help us. It's like a coin passed from one to another to another. Pass it on to somebody else. And visit us again sometime if you are ever in the area."

"We will," I replied.

We were ten feet from the door when I remembered something and turned back.

"Jed! Sorry. In the old garage by the road there's a car."

"A car?"

"Yes. It belongs to somebody in Eugene—"

"We'll make sure it gets back there," he answered, shaking his head.

"Thanks," I said and turned away, toward the trees and wilderness that would be our companions now.

A sadness welled up in me at leaving that cozy house and the goodness of Jed and Delia. When would I be able to rest again? I wondered. I looked at Loki, and it seemed like his mood was the same as mine. Xel seemed pensive too. I reached out and touched Loki's shoulder, ran my fingers through Xel's fur. They both looked at me, and I forced a smile.

"Let's go," I said. "Long walk ahead today."

CHAPTER 14

In the Mountains

All that day and all the next we walked along the old highway. It was impassable to any motorized vehicles in its state of disrepair, but it made a good walking path for us. A few times we saw floaters and airplanes off in the distance but none ever came near. Mostly, we saw trees—never ending forest, ferns, stones, gray sky, and rain. The river was our nearly constant companion.

Sometimes it looped off away from the highway, but it always came back around to meet us again. Most of the buildings and houses we passed were abandoned. Occasionally, we saw an inhabited homestead with smoke rising from the chimney and livestock in the fields but we steered clear. Maybe we would get lucky again and find people like Jed and Delia but it was too risky. We didn't want to take the chance.

They had given us several useful gifts when we parted: enough venison jerky and preserves to keep us going for a few days, herbal medicine for Loki, matches in a waterproof canister, and a bow and arrows. The bow was an old one that Jed restrung for us. He had made it himself—a simple arc of yew wood with notches for the animal sinew bowstring.

We walked about ten miles each day, going slowly and stopping in the early afternoon so that we could make camp and forage for our dinner. We both tried the bow, but it was Loki who finally hit a squirrel on the evening of our second day out. After that, I mainly let him do the shooting, but I did keep practicing in the afternoons, setting up targets and shooting arrow after arrow if it wasn't raining. He had experience with butchering from his time at the garage where they had raised chickens and eaten them. All members of the garage community were expected to learn all types of work. I didn't want to watch him gut the squirrel, so he carried it to the riverside and cleaned it while I built a fire. He managed to catch something most days after that.

It wasn't easy to find dry wood. We tried to camp near abandoned dwellings and old barns though, and I would gather as much wood as possible from inside them—floorboards, wall paneling, whatever I could find. I discovered I could dry kindling out with the lantern heater then throw the big pieces on once the fire was going. Xel, with his ability to access any information he needed, was always able to help us find edible plants and mushrooms. We didn't starve, but we were always hungry.

The nights were cold and silent except for the drip of rain on the tent, trees creaking in the wind, and sometimes the sound of small animals scurrying by. I slept well, tired from walking. We didn't talk very much. Xel and Loki seemed to look to me when decisions needed to be made. I had received the anonymous messages, and I had made the decision to travel to the coordinates given.

They were following along, hoping that my hunch was right. I couldn't say why, but I had a feeling that making this trek was the right decision. I was glad they trusted me. I barely trusted myself. I wasn't used to making decisions.

My parents, my teachers, and the other adults in my life had always just told me what to do. It was difficult. I was finding that along with responsibility comes worry. What if I was leading them into another trap? I went over the options in my head, mulling them over again and again as we trekked through that vast wilderness, but I could never come up with any better plan.

On the fifth night, we were laying in the tent with the never-ending rain plopping down on the roof in big drops from the tree branches above. We had finished Aeon's book the night before. I had many other books stored in the memory of my specs but I didn't want to power them up.

I was surprised by how quickly I had gotten used to not wearing them. We just lay quietly, thinking out own thoughts until it occurred to me that Loki had not been playing his shakuhachi flute since before our stay at Jed and Delia's house. In fact, he hadn't played since the night before we got to Eugene. I turned my head and saw his face in the lantern light.

His eyes were open, staring at the ceiling, his hands crossed on his chest.

"Loki, why haven't you played your flute lately?" I asked.

It took him a while to answer. Finally, still staring at the tent roof, he replied. "I haven't felt like it I guess. I have to be calm to play. At least a little bit. If you have a little bit of calmness, you can take it and build on it." He paused for several breaths then continued. "All I feel right now is afraid. I'm worried that I'm going to have another seizure and not come back this time. Maybe I'll just be a vegetable. What would you do then? You'd have to leave me behind so you could survive."

I felt a deep heart ache at his words. "That's *not* going to happen," I said. "We have the medicine Delia gave you."

"What if it doesn't work again? We're in the middle of nowhere."

"I'm sorry," I said. "Sorry I dragged you off into the woods. We're not going to leave you behind, though. We'll find somebody who can help. I have this feeling that when we get to the place of the coordinates, we'll find somebody who can help."

"I hope so," Loki said. "Sorry for being so pathetic."

"You don't have to apologize to me. I'm the girl who can barely control her emotions, remember?"

Loki looked over at me. "You say that, but it's not true. You're actually really good at controlling yourself. I can tell it's hard too. It's kind of scary when I see you going off, then you clamp it down. You get this look on you face like you could do anything you wanted, like nobody better stand in your way."

"Yeah," I answered, feeling the truth in what he said. "I guess I had to learn. It doesn't feel good to clamp it down though. The feeling doesn't go away. It's worse actually. I remember when I was a kid and I would melt down, I'd feel tired afterward but also calm, like I got something out I needed to get out."

Loki nodded. "That's sort of how I feel after a seizure. If I wake up after, anyway."

"We'll take care of you."

"I wish you didn't have to."

"You're strong, Loki. We wouldn't have made it this far without you. We would have been eaten by those rats or caught by the people in the sewer."

"I guess so," he said. "It just makes me feel weak and useless sometimes."

I didn't know how to answer him but Xel, curled at my feet, raised his head. "You are neither," he said. "The device in your head is evil. It was put there by evil people. If anything, you are amazingly strong to have survived this long with that thing in your brain. As Tara said, we would not have made it to this place without you. So, you are not useless either."

"Thanks," Loki said.

I could see and hear in his voice that he was choked with emotion.

"Let's go to sleep," I said, turning down the lantern. "More walking tomorrow."

❧❧❧

The next day, we came to a section of road that had been washed away by a mudslide. We climbed high up the hillside, above the tree line, and traversed the slide area there. It was tricky. We had to hop from stone to stone, crab walk down the cold, fog-damp sides of boulders, and plant our boots carefully in the exposed dirt and loose shale. Just as we were almost past the slide and ready to make our way back down to the road, I looked up and saw the silver glint of a floater in the distance. It was closer than any we had seen before, and it was moving toward us. I put my hand on Loki's arm and pointed. Xel had already seen it too.

"Let's get into the trees," I said, and we hurried down the slope. We reached the tree line and ran until the canopy covered us, hiding ourselves at the base of a big fir. We sat silently, backs against the massive tree trunk. My heart was beating fast. It had been days since I worried about being caught. I was sure we had evaded detec-

tion. Nobody should know where we were. The floater buzzed by, high above us, then turned and came back by closer to the ground. It passed over twice more, slowly. We crouched in terrified silence. Finally, it turned and flew away into the distance, disappearing over the crest of a foothill.

"They can't know we're here, can they, Xel?" I asked.

"It seems very unlikely," he answered, looking up at the gray sky.

"They can't track you, can they?"

"I have military grade encryption, and my data connection is direct to satellite so they should not be able to triangulate my location. They would be able to tell the general five-hundred-mile-or-so area where I am located based on the satellites I connect to. It may be best for me to limit my access to the net from this point on."

"Yeah, I guess so," I said. "Unless it's an emergency. What are we going to do now?"

"We'll have to walk in the forest," Loki said, "where they can't see us from above. It'll be slower."

"Yeah, I think you're right," I answered.

We spent the rest of the day bushwhacking through the woods near the road. It was tough going in the underbrush. We put our feet straight through rotten logs, tripped over hidden stones, and took long detours around blackberry brambles. By early afternoon, we were exhausted and ready to camp. Loki hadn't had any luck with the bow all day, and we didn't want to build a fire anyway so we chewed on the last of our jerky and opened the last jar of Delia's pickled beets.

Later, as I drifted off to sleep, I heard a long, plaintive cry in the distance. An answering cry came from another direction.

"What was that?" I asked.

"Wolves," Xel replied. "Calling to each other."

"There are wolves here?"

"Yes. They were extinct in this area for a hundred years but began to make a comeback early in the century."

The howls went on, back and forth, sounding sad but somehow hopeful at the same time. If the wolves could find each other across that great distance, maybe we could find our way too.

"I hope they don't decide to come after us."

"So do I," he said. "I think I can handle a wolf, though, if they do."

⃝ﾗⅇ⃝

It wasn't wolves we had to worry about the next day. We were close to the location of the coordinates and, perhaps, the end of our journey. I had lost track of the days, but it seemed like weeks since I had run away. Now, here I was in the middle of the Oregon wilderness with my companions, only miles away from what could be our last chance. Day after day of being on the run, hiding, looking out for danger had left me worn out to my core. Now, I felt equal parts trepidation and excitement like a current that crackled through me and leapt from the end of my fingers, making them tremble. We were all feeling it, all up early and itching to get started. Even Xel seemed anxious, pacing back and forth.

We passed the morning in frustration, fighting our way through the forest. Finally, around mid-morning, we stopped to drink from a small stream and rest on a fallen tree from which delicate ferns sprouted like antennae.

"How close are we now?" I asked, looking at Xel.

"Only three miles," he answered. "The coordinates are near an old ranch. It was a kind of resort hotel back in the teens and twenties where people would vacation but it has been abandoned for some time."

"If I hadn't run away, I'd be in science class right now," I said, shaking my head at how weird it was. "Jonas Johnson would be sitting next to me, and we'd be working on a lab project. Mr. Bhatia would be ignoring the students."

"Or maybe you would be at home, recovering from the operation on your brain," Xel said.

"True," I answered. "I shouldn't lose sight of why I ran in the first place. I haven't seen or heard that floater all morning. Do you think it's safe to walk on the road?"

I looked at Loki and Xel. Loki opened his mouth to answer but just then Xel jumped up on the log between us, eyes searching the sky above through the canopy.

"It's back," he said. "I can hear it. Pretty far away at the moment. We should keep moving, stay under the trees."

Loki and I silently hefted our packs. There was nothing we could do but keep on toward our goal. As we walked, casting nervous glances up at the sky, I noticed that there was more sky visible. The forest was starting to thin. As we continued on, the trees became smaller and more sparse. There were barren patches where few trees grew that we had to skirt around. I could feel that we were high up. We had been gaining altitude since we left Jed and Delia's homestead. The air was thin and cold and breathing was more difficult.

"We've reached the peak," Xel said, circling back and facing us. "From here, there will be less vegetation."

"The rain shadow effect," I said, remembering it from science class. Maybe I did learn something in science after all.

"Yes," he answered. "The rain falls on the western side of the mountain range as the clouds rise. The clouds are depleted once they reach the eastern side." He cocked his head, turning his ears. "The floater is approaching. Get down and remain still."

We ran to a large tree and crouched at its base. Once again, the airship passed over us slowly, then made a wide loop and passed by again. This time it slowed though and seemed to hover just above our position. The fear grew in me and I shivered, looking up at the metal belly of the floater a hundred feet above. Its four propellers spun almost soundlessly, blowing an icy wind down on us. The floater had no markings to indicate that it was a police vehicle. The more I looked at it, in fact, the more it seemed kind of old and beat up.

"What do we do?" I asked. "They know we're here."

"Run," Loki answered, pointing. "Run to those rocks over there. We can get behind them with the cliff to our backs. They'll have to land and come after us."

He was pointing to a pile of boulders a hundred yards away at the base of a cliff some fifty feet high. We would have to run across a meadow with no tree cover to get there. Still, I didn't have a better plan.

"Okay," I said. "Let's go."

We stood and ran as well as we could with the heavy packs on our backs. As soon as we broke from the cover of the trees, the floater passed over us and began to descend.

"It's going to cut us off," I yelled.

We came to a stop in the center of the meadow, panting in the thin air, as the floater came to rest on the ground before us. Xel stood in front, ready to spring. The rotors slowed, and the meadow grass which had been flattened by the wind slowly began to poke back up. I put my arm through Loki's, staying close to him as Xel backed up and leaned against my legs. There came a clank and the door on the side of the machine rolled open. A man stood in the opening, holding his hands up. He was dressed in old, well-worn clothes. They looked a lot like the surplus gear Loki and I were wearing—cargo pants, boots, a parka. He had a broad and open face. He took a deep breath, exhaled, and a cloud of condensed water vapor hung in the air for moment between us.

"Tara?" he called out. "Tara Rivers? I'm here to help. We sent you the message with the coordinates. We've been waiting for you."

I stood, dumbfounded, staring at the man. Was it possible? I hadn't ever pictured who or what we would find at the end of our journey into the mountains. I had been fixated on the goal of getting there. A guy in a beat-up floater wasn't what I expected, though. I didn't know what to say.

Xel took over for me though, relieving me of the need to speak. His voice rang out. "Who are you and why did you bring us here?"

"My name is Alphar," he answered. "I'm from a community near here. We know about the mind experiments TenCat Corp is doing. We warned you so you could get away. Gave you the coordinates so you could come here for help."

I turned half away, facing Xel and Loki. "What do we do?" I asked.

Loki was giving me a strange look. "I'm sorry, Tara, but I feel one coming on. It's going to be a bad one." He squeezed his eyes shut hard and pressed a hand to his forehead, swaying.

I turned back to the man in the floater. "Help me!" I called to him. "Loki needs help. He needs a doctor. Help me carry him."

CHAPTER 15

The Cedar Creek Commune

The man hopped down and rushed forward to help me with Loki. Together we carried him to the floater. I had begun to cry. I couldn't help it. All my emotions were boiling to the surface. I could barely concentrate on what was happening. I felt like the center of a top—the sharp point that makes contact with the ground. Everything was spinning around me in a blur. I must have helped get Loki up into the floater, but I didn't really remember it. When the spinning slowed down, I found I was in a chair. A harness was buckled, holding me in place.

Xel was next to me. He looked at me and squeezed his eyes. "It's going to be all right," he said.

Suddenly, the floater rose, banking to the right. The man was talking but I couldn't understand him. I saw the trees outside, a vast ocean of treetops stretching away, rippling into valleys, and climbing mountain sides. Rain spattered the window and was blown away. Down below was the road we had followed, meandering its way

through the trees. I saw a lake. I looked over and watched the man piloting the floater. He reached out and flipped a switch. Instrument panels glowed green and amber on the dash.

"Where is Loki?" I asked Xel.

"In a passenger seat behind you. He is strapped in."

I turned and looked. Loki was harnessed into a re-clined seat. He seemed to be sleeping.

"Where are you taking us?" I asked the man, strain-ing to speak loudly enough to be heard.

He looked over at me. "Cedar Creek Commune," he answered. "Our home. You'll see. It's not too far. You'll be safe there. We can get your friend medical help."

"He has a device in his brain," I said, feeling hollow. "He needs surgery."

The man stared at his hands on the flight controls for a moment, saying nothing, then lifted his eyes back to the windshield. "I'm sorry to hear that," he answered. "That's serious. He must be one of the early ones. We'll do what we can."

We flew for about twenty minutes in silence before we began to descend. There was a mountain ahead with a bald face of rock, boulders, and scree. As we got closer, I saw that there was a flat area like a step on the mountain-side. You couldn't see it until you were close. The man lowered the floater and landed it gently on the flat area. We were facing a sheer wall of rock. Small, gnarled trees twisted out of cracks and crevices

"What's this?" I asked. "I don't see anything."

"One moment," he said, holding up a finger then pointing at the rock face. There was a flicker and the stone disappeared, replaced by a massive hangar door that was rumbling open. "Hologram," he continued.

Beyond the door, I saw a big, high-ceilinged open space. A man and a woman, both in jumpsuits, ran out carrying cables and clipped them into recessed hooks on the front of the floater. There was a jerk and the floater began to move forward, drawn in by the cables. We rolled into the hangar and came to a stop.

As soon as we were inside, the man jumped up, went to the side door, and pulled it open. "We need medical," he yelled. "And get Yarrow. I have Tara Rivers. There's also a boy who's sick."

I fumbled with my harness and managed to unhook it. Loki's pack was on the floor with mine. I dug in the side pocket and found the bottle of medicine Delia had given us. It was a concentrated version of the tea she had made for him. With the bottle in hand, I crawled to the side of his chair and knelt.

"What's that?" the man asked.

"Herbal medicine," I replied. "It helps him when he has a seizure. He needs it."

I reached out and gently pulled his chin down, parting his lips. He was gaunt and his face was caked with dust and dirt. I was sure I looked the same. I hadn't had a shower since we ran from Wen's house. My hair had not been brushed for longer. It was a matted mess under my hat. Carefully, still holding his chin, I dribbled a few drops into his mouth. His body jerked, and he made a sour face at the taste of the tincture, but he seemed to relax a bit after that. I moved my hand to the top of his head, feeling his soft, short hair.

"You're going to be okay, Loki," I said. "We found them. We made it. They're going to help." I said the words, but I wasn't sure I believed them. I didn't know who to trust anymore.

"Tara?" The voice came from behind me.

I turned and saw a woman, stocky and strong looking with a lined face and gray hair pulled back. She wore a long, roughly knitted sweater and jeans. Behind her stood a slight man dressed in gray medical scrubs. "I'm Yarrow. This is Sky. He's a nurse. We need to take your friend to the infirmary and have a look at him. You come with me. I'm going to get you a meal, a bath, and a bed." As she talked, she directed her gaze to a point about two feet to my left. Even as disoriented as I was at that moment, the lack of any attempt at eye contact was unusual enough to startle me.

"His name is Loki," I said. "He needs help. He has an implant in his brain."

Yarrow nodded. "We're familiar with it. We'll do what we can. May I have the medicine? We will need to see what's in there." She reached out a hand, and I gave it to her. She passed it back to the other man, Sky, then held her empty hand back out toward me. "May I take your hand?"

I hesitated for a moment then reached out my hand, clasping hers.

She let go almost immediately. "Come along now. Your friend Loki will be looked after. They know what they're doing. The kitty can come with us. Come on, kitty. We'll get you a bath and a square meal, Tara. You've been on the road. Traveling in these mountains isn't easy."

I looked back at Loki. The pilot, Alphar, and Sky were unbuckling him. I stepped down out of the floater and Xel followed me. We watched as they carried Loki out and put him on a rolling stretcher.

"We'll let you know how he's doing. Don't worry, please," said Sky.

His voice was higher pitched than I expected. Something about his voice and his inflection made me think that my initial impression was wrong and Sky was actually female. Then I looked at him again and he looked like a man. My brain was tired and confused.

"I'm going to take care of him. Let Yarrow take care of you," he said, and they began to roll him away.

"Wait!" I called out. I ran to the side of the stretcher. "I can't just leave him."

"He's going to be okay," Yarrow said, standing beside me. "You're no use to him in your condition."

I reached out and touched his shoulder. "All right," I said. "Xel, will you go with them? Can he go with? And keep an eye on Loki."

Sky nodded his assent.

"I will protect him, Tara. Go with Yarrow. You need to eat and rest."

I watched them roll him away, hugging my arms across my chest. Xel followed—my two companions.

With a light touch on my shoulder, Yarrow led me to a big steel door across the hangar and from there into a concrete corridor with soft lights glowing in the ceiling. We stepped into an elevator and rode down. When the door opened, we emerged into a long, wide hallway. Walking slowly, we passed a large room where several people were seated at long wooden tables. Soft music was playing inside. A couple of the people looked up, and I just caught their glances as we passed. Another door just down the hallway led into a kitchen with stainless steel counters and industrial food preparation equipment. After that, we passed several closed doors. Yarrow stopped at one of them and pulled a ring of keys from her pocket. Inside was a storeroom with shelves of boxed food in cans and jars and instafood packs. Near the back was a shelf of neatly folded clothing—T-shirts, pants, socks, sweatshirts. Everything seemed broken in and neutral in color—gray, black, tan, white. Yarrow looked for a moment then selected a shirt, pants, socks, underwear, and a hooded sweatshirt. She also grabbed a pair of flip flops and a small mesh bag of toiletries.

"Not a lot of selection," she said, smiling, still looking somewhere off to my left. "We'll clean up your shoes. They look fine."

"What is this place?" I asked.

"Used to be a government base. They left it empty. We bought the land in an auction and took it over. That was years and years ago. We'll tell you all of it, the history. First, a shower and a meal." She led me out of the room, down the corridor, and into what looked like a locker room. There were metal cubbies on the wall and a wooden bench. The floor was white tile. "Showers are through the doorway there," she said, pointing. "Get cleaned up. I'll wait outside. Leave your clothes on the bench, and I'll take them to the laundry."

"My pack!" I said, remembering I had left it in the floater. It felt weird to be without it. It had been my constant companion for the past weeks.

"It will be brought to your room."

"My room?"

"Yes—I'll find a nice room for you. Don't worry. Take your time." She turned and walked out, the door swinging closed silently behind her.

I turned back to the bench where she had left the pile of clean clothes, neatly stacked. I saw that my boots had left dirty footprints on the floor so I sat and unlaced them. My head was spinning again. Slowly, I stood and peeled my filthy clothes off until I stood naked in the warm, humid air. There was a full length mirror on the wall by the doorway to the shower room. I approached it. I barely recognized myself. I was even thinner than before but hard muscles flexed beneath my skin where I had always been scrawny. My neck and face, my ankles, my wrists— everywhere my skin had been exposed—were dark with grime. I had a scratch on my cheek and a dark bruise on my thigh. My hair was almost in dreadlocks. My face was

gaunt and streaked where tears had run down my cheeks.
I turned away from my reflection, picked up the toiletries
bag, and walked through the doorway. There were six
individual shower stalls with curtains. I chose the nearest
and turned on the water. It came out cold but quickly
warmed. I stepped under the water, felt my knees buckle,
and lowered myself to the floor, sitting against the wall,
hugging myself, letting the rest of the tears I had been
holding back come.

It all seemed so sudden. I had gotten used to the days
of silence and walking in the woods. My mind had taken
on the rhythm of that life. Now I was somewhere else
again. Another place to learn. What was this place anyway? Who were these people? Would they really help
me? Why had they brought me here?

The questions swam in my head but after a little
while I began to calm. The warm water washed away my
tears and soothed me. Somehow, through the weeks of
being on the run, I had begun to find a new, deep reserve
of confidence and acceptance. I couldn't answer those
questions. Only time could give me answers. Whatever
the answers were, I would find a way to do what was
needed. I felt, again, as I had on the floater, that everything was spinning around me out of control. I was in the
eye of the storm. But deep inside me, at my core, I held
the still point, the center point—the strong, grounded center that supported the mass of the spinning world. Like
the words from the song I had heard in the car: *my spirit
stood on solid ground.* I could rely on it.

I sat on the wooden bench again, dressed in the
clothes Yarrow had given me. The clothing had no tags,
no branding, no itchy seams. The fabrics were soft and
worn in. There was no residue of perfumed detergent on
them. The soap and shampoo, too, had been unscented.
The toiletries kit included a brush which I was now using

with some of the conditioner to slowly untangle my hair. There was a knock at the door then, a moment later, Yarrow entered.

"Ah, cleaned up I see. Let's get some food in you. Salmon chowder and fresh bread in the dining room."

"How's Loki? Can I see him now?"

"Haven't heard from Sky yet. I'll go check on him while you eat." She was leading me back the way we had come. Soon we were at the large room by the kitchen. It was empty now but the music was still playing—soft, almost too quiet to hear, strings and piano. There was a long counter with an equally long, tall, open window looking into the kitchen next door. "Paul," Yarrow called, "We've got a customer. Give me big bowl of the chowder and some bread if you have any left."

A man in white came out of a walk in refrigerator at the back of the kitchen. "Coming up," he called back.

Moments later he reappeared with a tray holding a large, earthenware bowl and a thick slice of dark bread.

"Take that," Yarrow said, handing it to me. "Honey and butter over there," she said, pointing to a cupboard. "I'm off to check on your friend. Back in a bit. Eat well." With that, she turned and was gone again, through the door.

Paul was still there, behind the counter. "Good chowder," he said, gesturing toward the bowl. "Found some chanterelles yesterday. Fresh salmon too. Goat milk. Herbs from the garden. Bread's fresh out of the oven. Welcome to the commune." He was a big man with a round face. He spoke softly and avoided my eyes like Yarrow had.

"Thank you," I said and he turned away, back to his kitchen.

I seated myself at one of the long tables. The dining room was large with the same softly glowing lights as the

corridors, set into the high ceiling. There was an area toward the back of the room with a rag rug on the floor,
low, comfortable looking chairs, pillows, a sofa, and an
upright piano. The walls were painted a pale gray and
there was a large cork board with what looked like children's' artwork pinned neatly to it. I tried a spoonful of
the chowder and found that it was delicious. Before I
knew it, I was sopping up the final drops of soup with my
last crust of bread. Days of foraging in the woods had left
me half-starved. Just as I began to look around, wonder-
ing what I should do next, Yarrow came back into the
room.

"Clean and fed," she said in a singsong voice. "Now
we can go look in on your friend then off to bed with you.
Put your tray there. Paul will get it. That's right. Now this
way."

I followed along again as she led me out and through
a warren of passageways. We climbed a short set of
stairs, pushed through double doors, and turned into another room. This one, like all the rest, was windowless
but pleasantly lit. There were several beds and various
medical devices on carts pushed up against the walls. Sky
was bending over Loki who was on the bed closest to the
door. I walked over slowly. Xel was perched at the foot
of the bed, watching the readout on a monitor. As I
neared, I saw that Loki was covered with a blanket and
was wearing a thin circlet of plastic and metal on his
forehead.

"What's happening?" I asked.

Xel and Sky both turned toward me.

"Sky is monitoring Loki and attempting to determine
the extent to which the device has invaded his brain," Xel
answered. "Loki is resting but has not come around yet."

"I need Alphar and Oak," Sky said. "They know
about these devices. I'm not getting anywhere."

"I will ask them to come," Yarrow replied. "I'm going to take Tara to her room so she can get some rest."

"You should go get some sleep, Tara. I will keep watch." Xel said.

I reached out and put a hand on his back. "Thanks, Xel. Let me know if..." I broke off, yawning. I was exhausted. "...I don't know. Just please keep me updated."

"I will. Go sleep now. Loki is going to be okay."

⁊⁛⁊

When I woke, the room was dark, and I had no idea how long I had slept. Yarrow had led me, half-asleep, to the small room off a corridor near the kitchen and dining room. We had passed a few people on the way but Yarrow shushed them.

"Later. You'll meet everybody later," she had said.

I lay there for a while, snuggled down into the warm, soft blankets. After a little while, I remembered Yarrow had told me the room was outfitted with a simple computer.

"Computer," I said but the word came out as a croak. I cleared my throat and tried again. "Computer, what time is it?"

"Seven forty-two a.m.," a soft voice answered.

I had slept through the evening and all the way to the next morning.

"Please turn up the lights a little."

A soft glow filled the room, and I sat up, looking around. The room had a twin bed with a rust colored blanket, a wooden shelving unit with drawers, a small round rag rug like the one in the dining room, and a desk and chair.

"Yarrow has requested to be notified when you are awake. I will message her now."

"Okay," I answered. My bladder felt ready to burst. "Can you tell me how to get to the bathroom?"

When I came out of the bathroom, which was just down the hall from my room, I saw Yarrow coming up the corridor toward me.

"You're up," she said. "Looking rested. Your friend is still sleeping. Xel is with him. Interesting fellow, Xel. Had a good talk last night. Let's get breakfast then go see them. We need to have a talk with Oak. Explanations can wait until then. All questions answered after food and coffee."

The dining hall was crowded. There were about twenty people there, seated at the tables, eating oatmeal, toast, and eggs. People were talking but they spoke softly and the noise level was low. Yarrow ordered me a huge bowl of oatmeal and a mound of eggs. We sat down at the end of one of the tables next to a girl a couple of years younger than me and a man and woman who seemed to be her parents. Yarrow introduced me to them. The girl's name was Meadow, and her parents were Rex and Julie. Meadow glanced sidelong at me and smiled. She was small and plump with dark hair, cut short, and wore the same sort of clothes Yarrow had given me.

"May I speak to Tara?" Meadow asked very softly, eyes on her breakfast.

Yarrow gestured toward me. "Up to her, Meadow."

"Yes—of c—course," I stammered. "You don't have to ask permission."

"We always ask. Welcome to Cedar Creek," she said. "I'm going to help feed the goats after breakfast. It's animal day for me. Want to come?"

"Tara has some business after breakfast, Meadow," Yarrow said. "I'll bring her by later if she wants to meet the goats."

"Okay," Meadow answered, still smiling. "Mine is named Jonquil. She's white with black spots."

"She sounds pretty," I answered. "I'd love to come by and meet her."

Meadow took a big bite of toast with honey dripping from it.

I turned to Yarrow. "Why doesn't anyone make eye contact here?" I asked. "I mean—it's nice, actually. I'm just used to everybody always trying to get me to look at their eyes, though."

Yarrow nodded, chewing a bite of oatmeal.

"Some people don't like it," Meadow answered. Yarrow took a sip of coffee, waiting for her to continue. "We are taught not to do that unless we know somebody really well. Even then, we don't have to, if we don't want. Nobody expects it."

"Time to go, finish your toast," Meadow's father said.

Meadow was staring off into space, thinking about something.

He waited a moment then drummed his fingers lightly on the top of her head. "Finish your toast," he repeated. "Jonquil's waiting for you."

"Oh, yeah," Meadow said, shoving the last bite of toast into her mouth, and hopping up. She ran off without another word. Her parents stood too, nodded their goodbyes to me and Yarrow, and carried their trays to the counter.

"Nice people," Yarrow said. "Let's go see Loki and Xel."

Xel was curled at the foot of Loki's bed. Loki lay still, the device resting on his forehead, chest rising and falling rhythmically under the blanket. Xel stood when we entered. There was a woman in the room, sitting in the corner with specs on, she was quietly issuing commands and dictating. Next to her was an occupied bed I hadn't noticed on my previous visit. The occupant seemed to be a young woman. She was wearing a device similar to Loki's and lay absolutely still. Her face was pale and drawn and a knit hat covered her hair. I walked to Loki's bed. His face seemed younger, totally relaxed. They had bathed him. His face and hands were clean.

"He is still asleep, Tara," Xel said, rising. "They are controlling his brainwaves, keeping him in Delta. Alphar and Oak need to speak with us. They think you might be able to help."

"Okay," I said. "Let me just sit with him for a minute." I took his hand and held it, sitting on the edge of the bed. I was worried, and I had a tight feeling in my chest. I didn't want bad news, but I also wanted to know what was going on. After a couple of minutes, I stood. "All right," I said firmly, squeezing Loki's hand and then carefully placing it back down on the blanket, "let's go."

Yarrow led Xel and me to a room next door to the infirmary. Inside, one whole wall was covered by a bank of computer equipment. In the center of the room was a table with several chairs arrayed around it. Alphar sat at the table. He was wearing specs. Another man sat next to him—an older man with short gray hair and a neatly trimmed beard—also wearing specs. When we entered, they both turned to face us.

"Please come sit down," the gray-haired man said, gesturing to the empty chairs around the table.

"Tara, this is Oak, my husband," Yarrow said as we seated ourselves.

Xel jumped up onto the chair next to mine.

"Nice to meet you," I said, looking around the room.

"It's nice to meet you as well. I'm impressed that you made it here. Also, glad. We're happy to have you

here. I assume you have plenty of questions. Let me go ahead and explain who we are and what this place is."

I nodded. Like Yarrow, and everybody else at the compound, he wasn't looking directly at me.

"Yes, please," I answered. "I'd like to know. It was a long journey. It wasn't easy. Why did you send the messages to me? Why bring me here?"

"Yes, we've heard the story of your journey from your friend Xel. We're glad you decided to come." He leaned back in his chair, hands behind his head, and stared at the ceiling for a moment before continuing. "Let me begin at the beginning. Yarrow and I had a son, Joseph. He was everything to us. A beautiful boy. This was in the teens. Before the plagues and the floods and the reorganization. Our son was different. His brain didn't work in the normal way. The doctors told us he was autistic. Do you know the term? No, of course, you don't. It has been erased by the corporations. They control the curriculum in the schools, the psychology textbooks, everything. Well, back then, it was recognized. We studied and read and talked to experts and found out everything we could about it. There was a brief moment of enlightenment.

"There was a movement, a new civil rights movement, to grant people who were different, whose brains worked differently, full rights. The right to practical accommodations. Just as businesses were required to have ramps for people in wheelchairs and elevators were required to have braille for the blind, we worked to make society accept and meet the needs of neurodiverse people. Neurodiverse means having a brain that works differently from the norm. Our son had trouble in school. He was overwhelmed by the noise and the clutter in the classrooms. He couldn't stand the buzzing lights. He didn't understand the subtle, unspoken social cues that are such a major part of how children communicate with each other. Children and adults on the autism spectrum often have sensory issues. Noisy, crowded, bright, cluttered environments make it very hard for them to concentrate. They are prone to melt down or shut down when they're overwhelmed—basically becoming unable to regulate themselves. They have trouble reading facial expressions and body language. Sometimes they are highly verbal. Sometimes they barely speak at all. Some don't like to make eye contact. Some have gross motor impairment or sensory processing delays that can make them seem clumsy. Often, autistic kids have trouble making friends. They can be teased and picked on by their peers because of their difference..."

As he spoke I started to feel agitated. I felt blood rushing to my face. My legs twitched and I wanted to run. I held up my hand, squeezing my eyes shut, and he stopped speaking. It was like he was talking about me! All my issues, all my struggles. How did he know? I felt like I was in the psychologist's office again listening to them talk about me over the intercom. I flashed back to that moment and the anger and confusion I felt then returned full force. It was like I was back in that room. He knew everything. How could he know? I stood blindly and tottered for a moment, squeezing my hands into fists.

"I can't—need some air," I croaked, blundered my way to the door, threw it open, and ran down the hall. I kept going, not knowing where I was. I came to another door finally. There was daylight coming through a small window. I threw the door open, ran out, kept running for...I didn't know how long. The world around me was a blur.

Finally, I stopped. I crouched down, my chest heaving. There was dirt under my feet. Bits of straw were scattered in the dirt. I raised my head and looked around—an enclosed pen, like the goat pen at Jed and Delia's house. There was a goat ten paces from me. It bleated at me and walked away. *The still point*, I told myself, *I'm the still point. I'm the calm place inside the storm. I can handle this. How did he know about me though? No, he was describing his son, not me. A son who had the same problems I have. Another person like me.*

"Hi, Tara."

I turned and saw Meadow.

"Did you come to meet Jonquil?" she asked.

I looked at her for a moment. "Are you like me, Meadow?" I asked her back, returning a question for a question, not even sure what I meant.

Meadow seemed to know, though, even if I didn't. She nodded. "Do you mean autistic? Yeah. Maybe not just like you, though. We're all different, you know. We're all individuals. My dad told me you might not know about it. Is that true?"

"Yes, I guess so. I mean, where I'm from we didn't know about it. Or maybe some people did, but nobody told me. Is it really true?"

"Yeah. That's why we have this place. The commune. It's why my parents moved here with me. My thing is goats. And other animals. But mostly goats. I like them a lot. Did you know that goats have four stomachs? My parents are always telling me I talk about goats too much. I heard you have a cat. Can I meet him?"

"He's not a real cat," I said, smiling at Meadow's enthusiasm. "He's a robot." Something about her grounded me. I felt something click into place in that moment. There were other people like me. Meadow, standing in front of me, was a person like me.

"Is that him?" she asked, pointing.

I turned and saw Xel sitting on a fence post next to a

gate I had apparently left open. A couple of goats were hanging around. They looked like they wanted to make a dash for the open gate but they also looked like they didn't want to get too close to Xel.

"Yes," I answered. "His name is Xel. I think I have to go back. Do you want to meet him right now, before I go? I can come back later and meet Jonquil."

≈≈≈

"I'm sorry, Tara," Oak said when Xel and I returned to the room. "I should have taken that slower. I forget sometimes what it is like out there in the world you came to us from. I know it must be difficult. You have held this in all your life. You've felt different but you haven't been able to explain it. Am I correct?" I nodded and he continued. "It had never been acknowledged until you overheard the doctors telling your parents you had a disease— a disease that needed to be cured by putting a device in your head. We don't believe in that here. We're fighting against it. That's why we sent you the messages and hoped you would find your way to us."

Oak told me the history. For a while things got better. They were able to get help for their son. Accommodations were made. The children at his school were educated to understand why he and other kids like him were different. They were taught to accept difference. But then the country took a turn. New people came to power who did not believe in education and accommodation and diversity. They took away the funding. They put bureaucrats in charge. They turned power over to the corporations, and corporations didn't like difference. They wanted to stamp it out. Good workers and good consumers were predictable. Corporations put a lot of emphasis on culture. Everybody had to fit into the corporate culture, had to be a team player. When Oak and Yarrow saw how things were going, they decided to move away, into the country. They bought land in the mountains. They invited a few others to come with them and they set up their own community. It took years but they turned the old, decommissioned military base into a home. Now their community had over fifty people. It was like Loki and Aeon's garage but in the mountains. They grew and gathered their own food, made their own clothes, kept the old base maintained and upgraded it when necessary.

"Now, though, we come to the troubling part, Tara," Yarrow said, taking over. "Our son was very good with technology. He loved computers and electronics. He wasn't happy with the life we live here. He wanted to go out into the world and see what it was like in other places. He went to work for one of the corporations. I bet you can guess which one."

"TenCat," I said.

"Yes," she continued. "He has been there for several years. It's a struggle. He has to hide his difference. I think you know how exhausting that is. We call it masking."

I nodded.

"The last straw, though, was when he found out about a secret program TenCat had developed," she continued. "The brain implants. Meant to cure people whose brains didn't work the way TenCat wanted them to."

"Loki," I said.

"Yes. In the beginning, they kidnapped children. Homeless children who would only be missed by their parents who were powerless, who no one would listen to. They perfected the device. It's very effective now and safe in most cases. However, as you suspected, it changes the children. It makes them docile. It makes them easy to control. We believe it's wrong. People like me, like my son, like Meadow who you met earlier, like you, maybe—we're not broken. We don't need fixing. We need acceptance. Some things are harder for us but some things are easier. We tend to have very good memories. We tend to be detail oriented and good at thinking about systems. Sometimes we see things from a different perspective. We can have insights other people miss."

"But how did you know about me? About my situation?"

"Our son is still there, Tara," Oak said. "When he found out what they were doing, he decided to stay. He has gained access to the medical records. He knows what they're planning and who their targets are. He has to be very careful. He warns kids by sending anonymous messages. He directs them to us. He hates it there, but he stays so that he can help. If they found out what he's doing, it could be very serious."

"So it's your son who helped me escape," I said, "who sent me the messages."

"Yes."

"But what about Loki? Can you help him?"

Oak and Yarrow were silent. Then Alphar spoke. "None of us are doctors, Tara. Sky is a nurse. We would need a very skilled surgeon to remove the device. Even then, we don't know if it would help him or kill him. Did you see the other occupant of our infirmary? Her name is Keira. Joseph brought her to us almost a year ago. She's another victim of the TenCat doctors. The implant in her brain is similar to Loki's. We have been keeping her in a medically induced coma almost since she arrived." I looked down at my hands. Tears filled my eyes. I seemed to be crying at every turn.

"But we have an idea, Tara," Oak said.

I looked up. "What? What idea?"

"We will need your help. It could be dangerous."

"I'll do it," I said. "I don't care what it is. I want to do it."

CHAPTER 16

The Plan

I sat in the room Yarrow had assigned to me, on the bed, back against the cool wall. Xel sat next to me. We had been sitting there silently for a while, thinking. One of the things I liked best about Xel was that he never felt the need to make idle conversation. Finally, I felt like I was ready to talk it out. "Explain it to me again please, Xel."

"Tara, I don't like this plan. I don't think we should bother considering it. It's too dangerous."

"I know how you feel, Xel, but I have to decide for myself."

He sat for a moment then began going over the details again. "The basic goal is to get the firmware source code for the implant device. If we have the source code, we can rewrite it. We can make the device stop interfering with Loki's brain. Keira's too. Oak and Yarrow's son Joseph does not have a high enough clearance at TenCat to access the source code. He has managed to access the patient records for the project without being detected, but he has not been able to hack into the systems holding the source code. Your father is a higher-level employee and does have access to those systems. The plan, which I feel is too risky, is for you to travel back to Los Angeles, go to your family's apartment at night, and use your father's specs to download the source code. Joseph works in the operations control department. He has access to the system that controls the apartment blocks and is able to see that they have not disabled your biometric profile yet. You will be able to enter the building by facial recognition at the door. He will take the house computer offline so that it will not be able to alert your family or the authorities of your presence. Theoretically, you will be able to walk right in. However, that does not mean you will be able to successfully use your father's specs. They are locked to his biometrics. You would need him to unlock them with an eye scan or his fingerprint."

"His specs are trained to my fingerprint. At least, I think they are. We were playing around one night, and he set me up. My sister too. He might have erased it, though. Even if he did, he's a really sound sleeper. You know he usually falls asleep in the chair in his office. He stays up half the night working. I can just hold the contact on his finger to unlock them."

"Too risky, Tara. So many things could go wrong."

"How would I get to LA?"

"You would be taken to the border by floater. From there, someone, a friend of Joseph's, would pick you up and you would go by car."

I was silent for another minute, thinking about it. "I'm not going to lie," I said finally. "The idea of going back there is really scary. We just made it here. I can't let them just keep Loki in a coma forever, though. Like that girl Keira. What kind of life is that? I need to think about this. I'm going to go help Meadow with the goats. I told her I'd come back. I need time to think."

I found a red-cheeked Meadow still out in the goat pen. She was working with a large, capable-looking woman in overalls who appeared to be trimming a goat's hooves.

Meadow stood in front of the goat and distracted it by waving her arms and chattering while the woman stood behind and carefully trimmed the back left hoof with a pair of shears. I waited patiently while they worked, watching. When they were done, the woman let go of the goat's leg, and it dashed off at once, jumping and bleating.

Meadow saw me and walked over. "That's Hugin. He's a pygora. That's a cross between a pygmy and an angora. We raise them for the hair. We shear them twice a year, and then Sabrina uses the hair to make yarn for sweaters, scarves, and mittens."

"Who's Sabrina?" I asked.

"Oh, she's the seamstress. She makes all the clothes we wear here. She made your clothes." Meadow gestured at the clothes Yarrow had picked out for me. "A lot of people here have issues with commercial clothes because they have scratchy tags and fabrics, or they don't fit right. So Sabrina makes clothes for us. You can have your own clothes too if you want. There's no rule about not wearing stuff from outside. Most people wear hers, though, because they're so comfortable and nice looking." The woman who had been trimming the goat's hooves waved to Meadow. "Oh! Sorry. This is Talya. She is in charge of the goats. I'm learning from her."

"Nice to meet you. I'm Tara," I said.

Talya hung back, looking at the ground off to my right, nodding and smiling.

"Talya doesn't talk," Meadow said. "She can communicate with a tablet though. Or with specs. We don't use specs here very much though."

Talya waved again and wandered off toward a shed across the pen. I looked around. We were in a clearing in a wooded valley. It was cold out but not raining for once. A hundred yards away was a doorway leading back into the mountain and the warren of tunnels and rooms that made up the commune.

"Do you have time to talk?" I asked. "I don't want to keep you from work you're supposed to be doing."

"No, it's fine. Oak and Yarrow told me I should help you out and show you around if you came by. Do you want to go for a walk? Just up the hill there's a nice view."

"Okay," I answered.

I wasn't sure I really did want to go for a walk. I'd had enough of walking for a while, but once we hopped over the fence and started up the hill, it felt good to be moving. There was a narrow path through the trees, and we walked slowly. Meadow led the way.

"How long have you lived here?" I asked.

"Two years," she answered. "I used to have trouble in school. Other kids picked on me. My parents knew someone who had heard about the commune from another friend. It's all word of mouth. They don't advertise that they're out here. Anyway, we came here and checked it out. I liked it right away. My dad did too. My mom wasn't sure, but we convinced her."

"Does everybody have a job here?" I asked.

We had reached the crest of the hill and both sat down on a log at the top, looking out over wooded hillsides and mountains towering in the distance.

"Yeah, everybody helps do the work. Stuff like cleaning and washing dishes and laundry or whatever is all scheduled, and we all help. Most people have a specialty, though. Like Talya. She's the goat keeper. Sabrina makes clothes. My dad is a mechanic so he helps with all the machinery and plumbing and electrical stuff. My mom teaches in the preschool."

"There's a school here?"

"Yeah. There are seventeen other kids. All ages. We just have two rooms for classrooms. It's pretty weird. I mean, we used to live in a house, like normal. I went to school, and my parents had normal jobs where they got paid by the cluster government. Then we moved here. Oak says people used to live in communes a lot back in the nineteen sixties and seventies. Then it went out of style, I guess."

"Yeah, I heard that too. My friend Loki lives in a kind of commune I guess. So it's not that weird. Wait, if there's a school here, why aren't you there?"

"I am. Well, not right this minute. We're going for a walk." She grinned. "But learning about the goats from Talya is part of school. We all get to pick stuff we like and learn more about it. I spend one day a week working with Talya so I can learn how to take care of the goats."

"Cool. I mean, sounds like something I would like. I don't like school very much."

"I didn't either, until I came here. You could go to our school. I mean, if you're going to stay here at the commune. Sorry, I'm not supposed to ask you any questions about your parents or anything like that."

"I know. Sorry. I'm not supposed to talk about my situation right now. I can tell you later, maybe. I want to see your school, though. Will you show me?"

"Yeah, we should go get lunch now, though. It must be almost time. After lunch, I can show you around the whole place."

We walked back down the hill, through the goat enclosure where Meadow introduced me to her favorite

goat, Jonquil, and then on into the commune. There were people in the hallways and corridors, all heading the same direction as us more or less.

We all congregated in the dining hall where they were serving lunch.

"Oh, good, Paul's cooking today," Meadow said when she saw him in the kitchen. "I always get a stomach ache when Sergio cooks. Paul cooks most of the time. Sergio only cooks when Paul is taking a day off."

The meal was thick vegetable soup with more fresh bread. We got our trays and found a place at one of the crowded tables.

"What do people do if they don't like the food? Like, if I hated vegetable soup?"

"Oh, everybody can make their own food if they want. Judith over there—" Meadow motioned with her head without looking, "—she eats the same thing every day. Peanut butter and jam sandwiches. She just doesn't like anything else. She has to take vitamin supplements."

"Where does the peanut butter come from? Do people have to go out and shop? How do you buy stuff?"

"We make some products here that we sell. We make beer and honey. We have bees. I'll show you the hives. We also do software development. There are a few people who are good at programming, and they live here and work for clients on the outside. Alphar does that."

I nodded, thinking about the commune. It was a weird place but it seemed like it worked. And they had saved me. "Who's in charge? I mean, who makes decisions about stuff?"

"All the adults get together and talk when they have to make a decision. Oak and Yarrow started the commune so people respect them and listen to them, but everybody gets to vote in the end. It's a democracy like the United States used to be before the reorg."

I looked around at all the people in the room. "Is everybody...like you and me?"

"Neurodiverse? No. Some people are neurotypical and just came here because of their kids. Like my parents. Oak and Yarrow started the commune for their son. So they could get him away from a bad environment. It's a good place for everybody, though. I think it helps everybody to be in a place where we focus on meeting people's needs. We were talking in school yesterday about equity. That means giving everybody what they need to be successful." Meadow's voice got a little shaky, and she rocked in her seat and nodded her head as she talked. "Before we came here, it was bad for me. In school, they treated me like I was stupid or I was acting out intentionally. Other kids were mean to me. Now, I like school. I'm still not very good at making friends, though."

"I'm bad at making friends too," I said. "I only have one friend. Other than Xel and Loki, but they're more like brothers or something. I'll probably never get to see my one friend again."

"Maybe we can be friends," Meadow said, still rocking, looking at her hands in her lap.

"Yeah, I think we should be," I answered. "We definitely should be."

After lunch, we walked around the commune. Meadow showed me the beehives which looked like white wooden crates stacked on top of each other. They were in a clearing near the goat enclosure. Next, we walked back through the commune and she showed me the laundry facility, the brewery where they made the beer they sold, the maintenance room where we found her father disassembling and cleaning a motor, the fusion plant where the electricity for the commune was generated, and finally, the school. The school rooms were right next to each other and they had sharply sloped ceilings—high at the side where we entered and lower at the far end. Like most of the rooms in the commune, they didn't have windows since they were underground. The students were still having lunch and were all gathered in one of the rooms. We looked into the empty room next door. A beautiful glow seemed to be coming right through the ceiling and illuminating the room. Meadow explained that we were at the edge of the mountain and that the ceilings were made from translucent concrete with optical fibers that allowed the sunlight to pass through. On the outside it was textured to look like rock. Oak and Yarrow tried to disguise the commune from the outside as much as possible to make it look like just a small family homestead. They didn't want a lot of windows that would show the extent of the tunnels and rooms under the mountain. The translucent concrete was something new they were trying out. It was an idea brought to them by a family who joined the community a few years before.

The warm glow from the ceiling illuminated a large classroom without desks or any obvious focal point. The room had nice wooden shelves and cubbies, a few tables with chairs against the walls, and lots of pillows and carpets on the floor for lounging. There was no clutter, no posters covering the walls, everything was neatly organized and put away. I noticed a sort of hammock suspended from the ceiling by ropes and pointed to it questioningly.

"Some kids like to swing. The feeling of movement helps them," Meadow answered. "There's a quiet room over there too," she said, pointing to an open door that led into a small room with a comfortable chair. "Kids can go in there when they are feeling overwhelmed."

We spent some more time looking over the room. Soon after we arrived, the younger students began to drift back in through an adjoining door. Meadow's mom came in with them.

"They're doing computer science next door. Alphar's teaching today. You might enjoy seeing it," she said.

We went and stood in the doorway. There were about seven kids in the older class, all younger than me. Meadow was the oldest of the school-aged kids at the commune. The students were wearing specs and sitting in a circle on the floor. One of the students, a skinny boy with dark hair, was speaking.

"I'm not sure I get it. When I ran it, I got twenty-eight comparisons."

Alphar looked around the circle. "Can anyone think of why that might be?" He waited a moment then saw me and Meadow in the doorway. "Meadow, Tara. We're going over selection sort versus quicksort algorithms. Can either of you explain why John might get that result?"

I did some quick mental math. "Are you sorting eight objects?" I asked. Alphar nodded, smiling. "He probably randomly chose one on either end of the distribution," I continued. "If you get one of the six in the middle, quicksort will only take fourteen comparisons. It's never worse than selection sort but usually better."

"Thanks Tara," Alphar said. "Exactly right. Maybe you should be teaching this class."

ᘓᕙᘓ

That evening after dinner, I said goodbye to Meadow when she left to go to bed. I remained in the dining hall with Oak and Yarrow. Xel sat at my side. The majority of the adults also stayed behind. The tables were moved to the edges of the room and we made a big circle of the benches. It was meeting night, and I was the topic.

Once everyone was seated and quiet, Yarrow spoke. "Let's begin with silence," she said and closed her eyes.

Everyone else also closed their eyes and bowed their heads so I did too. We sat like that for a minute or two, then I heard Oak clear his throat.

"Computer, please begin recording," he said. "Archive this as meeting twelve of the current year. This meeting has begun. We are here tonight to discuss the program we have been running to help neurodiverse kids escape the brain implants TenCat has invented. When we heard from Joseph and then when he brought Keira to us, we agreed to allow him to send anonymous messages to kids who might be in danger. We didn't know whether anyone would make it here or even try, but we decided to risk it. Now we have our answer. Tara Rivers made it here, against harsh odds. She brought with her Loki, another child like Keira, used by TenCat and then tossed aside. She also brought her cat Xel. I sent all of you an abstract of the plan we have devised to get the firmware code for the brain implants. The plan rests on Tara. Tara's father has access to the code. Tara has access to her family's apartment. Her voice and face can get her into the building. Tara has been considering our plan." Oak looked at me. "Have you decided, Tara?"

"Yes," I answered.

"Please speak," Yarrow said.

I looked around the circle. I saw a few familiar faces—Meadow's parents; Paul, the cook; Talya, the goat keeper; Alphar. They were all looking politely at the floor, listening for my answer. Blood rushed to my face and my stomach churned. I took a deep breath. "I want to go," I said. "I want to help Loki. I can't leave him like that."

Xel placed a paw on my hand. "If you go, I will go with you," he said.

I nodded my agreement.

"This will be dangerous. Are you sure?" Oak asked.

"Yes," I replied.

"Fine then. We will make arrangements. We need to move fast. They might disable your access to the apartment block at any time."

"I would like to ask a question," someone said.

I looked around and saw a man I didn't recognize at first. Then I realized he was a man we had met in the brewery. "How do we know she isn't a spy—someone TenCat sent to infiltrate us?"

There was a low mumbling from the group.

"It's a fair question," Alphar said. "I think we can be pretty sure TenCat doesn't know about us, though. If they did, they would neutralize Joseph first. Also, a spy would not have brought Loki, another victim of the brain implant program."

There was more mumbling.

"Any other questions or concerns?" Oak asked.

We all waited a moment but no one responded.

"One more question, Tara," Yarrow said. "You came to us on the run, out of the woods, with a sick companion. You have been with us only a couple of days. Do you intend to stay? Would you like to live here with us? I don't expect you to answer now," she said, holding up a hand. "Think about it. If you choose to stay, you will have to have a new identity, a new name."

"Thanks," I answered. "Thanks for taking us in and helping us. I'll think about it, and I'll give you my answer if we make it back."

❧❧❧

Before bed I went by the infirmary to check on Loki. He lay there under a light blanket, chest rising and fall-

ing. I normally didn't see faces as a whole very well, maybe because I tended to focus on individual characteristics. But because he had his eyes closed, maybe also because I was in an unusual mental state, preoccupied with the task ahead of me, I found myself really seeing his face for the first time. He was handsome. His features were beautiful and regular and well balanced. I felt, for a moment, the shiver I had felt before when I touched his hand or lifted him. He was more to me than I had admitted to myself. I had thought of him as a brother but I knew now that I wanted him to be something else. I pushed the thought away. First I had to get the code. Only then could we try to save him. I curled my fingers in his hand.

"I'm going to go get it, Loki," I whispered. "You're going to be okay. I'll come back. I promise."

CHAPTER 17

Going Back

I t took a full day for Oak, Yarrow, and Alphar to get everything ready and make the necessary arrangements. I spent the day pacing in my room, taking a long walk in the woods with Xel and Meadow, pacing some more, and finally eating dinner and then going to my room early. Before I went to bed, though, I organized my backpack. I transferred a few items I might need from Loki's pack to mine, leaving most of the heavy and bulky things and just taking what I thought would be useful. Finally, I lay down in bed and asked the computer to dim the lights.

"Tara," Xel said. "I still think this is a bad idea."

"I know," I answered. "It might be. We might get caught. I wouldn't be able to live with myself if I didn't go though. Are you ready?"

"Yes."

"Me too. I'm glad you're coming with me."

Sleep took a long time to come. I lay still, thinking about everything that had happened since I decided to run. It didn't seemed real. I thought about my parents. What were they thinking? How were they feeling? Did they feel guilty? Or did they still think they were doing the right thing? I wondered if my running away had endangered their jobs or made their lives harder. I had spent a lot of time thinking about my childhood and my parents over the last days and weeks. I didn't hold any grudge against them. They were just doing what they thought was right. What if they had been more like Meadow's parents, though? I had the same trouble in school as Meadow. I was teased, picked on, bullied, and friendless until I met Rosie. The school environment was hard for me to deal with. There was too much noise, too much chaos. The teachers talked fast and got annoyed when I asked them to repeat things. If my parents had known about Cedar Creek Commune, would they have considered moving? I didn't think so. They had jumped at the chance to move south, out of the rogue cluster, and have high-class, well-paying jobs and a luxurious life. They probably thought they were doing it for me and Zoie— trying to give us a better life. Zoie might be happy there, but I was better off at the commune. I liked the calm environment; the slow pace of life; the steady, thoughtful people; and nature all around us, instead of concrete. Something about being in nature made me feel alive, accepted, and whole in a way the city never did. If Xel and I made it through, I would come back. I would take on a new name, a new identity, and become a new person.

ひとつ

In the morning, I ate an early breakfast with Alphar and Xel. The dining room was empty except for us. Paul was in the kitchen, cooking and getting ready for the breakfast rush.

We ate in silence, listening to Paul clanking pots and pans around. I was back in my army surplus traveling gear and had my backpack with me.

Alphar sat back, patting his belly. "You know your stuff with computer programming," he said. "Your answer the other day was right on."

"Tara reprogrammed my firmware," Xel said. "I have tried to examine the code but I find the exercise distasteful. It feels wrong since it is the code that runs my brain. Nonetheless, I feel that she did quite a good job."

"I agree," Alphar answered. "If you bring back the firmware code, I'll need you to help me figure it out."

"I'll do what I can," I said. "Do you really think we can do it?"

"Yes. If you can get it, we can hack it. Ready to go?" I nodded. "Okay," he said. "Let's go fire up the floater."

The flight to the border didn't take long. It was a beautiful, sunny day. I watched the scenery flow by below—endless forests and lakes and rivers. The floater had an old fashioned radio that had been ingeniously inserted into the instrument panel. Shortly after we took off, Alphar turned it on, and an old country western song began playing. I glanced at the frequency read-out and it seemed to be close to the one I had picked up in the car when we drove out of Eugene.

"I wonder if that's the same station?" I said.

"What's that?" Alphar asked.

"When we escaped from Eugene, we were driving into the mountains on old Highway One-Twenty-Six, and I turned on the radio. It picked up a station playing country music songs. It was the only station I could find."

"I don't doubt it," Alphar said. "Nobody broadcasts radio anymore. Except me."

"Except you?"

"Yeah—that's my station. I have a transmitter at the

commune. I built it myself. I like broadcasting even if there's nobody listening."

I nodded, enjoying the music. "I hope we make it back and I get to listen to your station again."

"I hope so too, Tara. It doesn't seem right just dropping you off and sending you back there by yourself."

"There's no other option. Besides, I have Xel. We'll make it through together."

Alphar dropped us off two miles from the border in a wooded area. We stood in a small clearing and watched the floater rise, bank, and shoot off back toward the north. We were supposed to hike the two miles and meet our contact just across the border on old US Route 97. She would be waiting for us in a hacked autocab. I stood for a moment, listening to the sound of the wind blowing through the trees. The world was spinning around me again, I thought, remembering the song from that night on the road when we were running from Eugene and another betrayal. But the ground was solid beneath my feet and my spirit was planted there. If nothing else, I could take a step forward. I picked up my pack and put my arms through the straps.

"Let's go, Xel," I said. "We need to try to make good time."

We followed an old, overgrown trail through the forest. The walking was not hard. I was in good shape, maybe for the first time in my life. The air was chilly but my clothes kept me warm. The farther we went, though, the more trepidation I felt about going back. I felt like, by running away, I had made a clean break. I had left behind my old life, my family, my home, and started on something new. Going back felt wrong. It was something I needed to do, though, and not just for Loki. If I could make it there and stand in my room in my family's apartment one more time, look at my parents' and my sister's sleeping faces, I could know for sure whether or not I had made the right decision. I envisioned myself there as we walked. I knew that the answer would come.

We emerged from forest into a terrain of low hills with scrub oak and tall grass. Twenty minutes later, cresting a hill, we saw the highway below cutting across our path. It was about two hundred yards away.

"How's our location?" I asked.

"We are in good shape," Xel answered. "The coordinates set for our rendezvous are just ahead. Perhaps we should rest here, out of sight, until we see the car arrive."

"Good idea. Are we early?" I asked, dropping my pack in the grass and seating myself on it.

Xel leapt up onto a rock and sat, surveying the road. "Yes," he answered. "We are twenty-three minutes ahead of schedule."

"How come they keep this highway maintained? Are there towns around here that are still inhabited?"

"Klamath Falls still has a small population. This highway is the only way to get there. There's very little traffic."

We sat for a while. I watched a hawk high above, circling, looking for breakfast. Finally, Xel's ears pricked up, and he turned to the east.

"I hear a vehicle approaching," he reported.

A minute later, I saw the car coming. It was a highway cruiser—more spacious than the autocabs that provided transport in the cities. Highway cruisers could be booked for short trips between metro areas. People generally flew when they traveled farther. The car slowed and pulled to the shoulder. The door closest to us slid open and a woman stepped out. She was tall and dressed in black jeans, a black jacket, and high boots. She stood by the car, shading her eyes and looking around.

"I guess we just have to trust," I said and stood up, waving my arms.

Xel followed me down the hill. The woman saw us and waved. When we got to the car, she gestured for us to enter, looking around to make sure we were not observed. I climbed in, slid across the smooth seat, and Xel followed. The woman jumped in after us and pushed a button to close the door.

"Continue to the programmed destination," she said. Her voice was low and she had a slight accent. The car rolled back onto the road and accelerated. "I'm glad you made it, Tara. I'm Celeste. I'm going to get you to LA."

The interior of the car was spacious with seats facing each other. She sat across from us. I thought she was very beautiful. Also, she seemed cool and self-assured.

"Thanks," I answered. "This is Xel. Do you know Joseph? Oak and Yarrow's son?"

"Yeah, he's my friend. We work together. A small group working against the corporation."

"You work at TenCat too?"

"No. I'm a freelance programmer. I mainly do crypto. I meant we work together on other kinds of projects."

"Did you hack this autocar?"

"We worked on the code together. This is the first time we've tried it."

"So, we're safe taking it all the way to LA?"

"I hope so. We should be. As I said, first time we've tried the hack. It's invisible to the controller system but should check out if anybody scans it. You are doing a very brave thing, Tara. We've been trying to get the implant firmware code for over a year. We've all been working on it but the TenCat system is very well protected. If you're successful it will be a big help."

I swallowed hard, looking out the window. "I hope I can help," I said. "I'm trying to be brave."

Celeste nodded, looking straight at me. I met her eyes for a moment then looked away.

"Sorry," she said. "Joseph doesn't like looking me in the eyes either. I always forget. I'll help you out as much as I can. Joseph will help too. He'll be monitoring the systems in the building."

"I'll be there too," Xel said.

"The drive will take about seven hours," Celeste said after a few moments of silence. "Would you like something to eat?"

ↄ◌ↄ

Outside of Sacramento there was a roadblock. Traffic slowed to a crawl. We were surrounded by tall trucks like the one we had stowed away on when we made the trip north. In the shadow of the trucks, I suddenly felt trapped. My heartbeat quickened, and I looked at Celeste who was engrossed in some activity on her specs.

"What's going on?"

"Looks like a checkpoint. They've been doing this lately, searching for people traveling illegally." She pulled a bag from under the seat, dug through it for a moment, then withdrew a small device. "Hold out your arm. No, the other one. Yes. There it is," she said, pulling the metallic tube down to my wrist and exposing my biosensor. The device was a solid block of plastic with a silver square on the bottom. She pressed the square to my forearm, covering the biosensor. I felt a tingle for a moment, then Celeste removed the device and put it away.

"What is that?"

"One of Joseph's inventions. It reprograms the chip. You have a new identity now. You're my younger sister. Your name is Lake." She handed me an identity card. "If they ask questions, we're traveling to visit our mother in

Los Angeles. Sorry, I didn't want to reprogram your chip if it wasn't necessary."

"That's okay," I answered. "I'm pretty much used to the fact that I can't go back to my old life. What about Xel?"

"You'll have to hide," Celeste answered, looking at Xel. She leaned forward and reached under her seat. She pulled on something and a panel fell open. "Secret compartment. Faraday cage. We thought of everything. Hurry inside. We'll let you out as soon as we're through."

Xel prowled forward, crouched, and curled himself into the compartment.

"Thanks, Xel," I said. "It's just for a few minutes."

When we got to the front of the line, a woman in the dark gray uniform of the security forces approached our vehicle. Celeste opened the door.

"Wrists and cards," the woman said, her voice distorted by her respie. Celeste held hers out and the woman scanned it. I hesitated for a moment, feeling my skin prickle with nervous fear, then held mine out. She scanned mine, looked at some readout on her specs for a moment, then nodded.

"Move along," she said and pressed the button to close the door. The car accelerated and I exhaled, realizing I had been holding my breath the whole time. I sat back for a moment, eyes closed, breathing deeply. I felt Xel hop onto the seat next to me.

"Are you all right, Tara?" He asked.

I nodded, keeping my eyes closed. After a few minutes I felt calm. "Why do you have a biosensor?" I asked Celeste. "You're not required."

"No. They're actually easier to hack than the old cards, though. I went ahead and got one so I could change my identity if needed."

I was feeling sleepy, having gotten up early and gone

to sleep late, so I reclined my seat and turned my head to watch the scenery go by. There wasn't much to look at but the broad sides of trucks as we passed them, clouds in the blue sky, farmland that had returned to its wild origins. Everything seemed to blur and float apart into pixels as I squinted my eyes. I felt for a moment like I was seeing into some deeper reality. The world was a collection of dust motes. The motes danced and made patterns and those patterns were our lives. One moment the patterning put me in Ms. Laughlin's programming class at PVC-STEM. The next moment I was on the run in a sewer tunnel under the ground. Next, I was in the woods in the middle of nowhere, walking. Thinking through those memories, reliving them in my mind's eye, I grew drowsier. I yawned. My eyes felt heavy so I closed them. Pretty soon, I fell asleep.

When I woke up, we were just entering Los Angeles. We passed by the glittering downtown then zipped over what I now knew were mostly empty, deserted neighborhoods crumbling into decay. I drew a ragged breath as I looked out over the cityscape. I hadn't thought I would ever come back, certainly not so soon.

"We'll go to my place and wait until it's time," Celeste said. "It's good you had a nap."

Celeste lived in an old brick warehouse building in an area west of downtown called Koreatown. Most of the other buildings on the block were derelict but Celeste explained to me that the warehouse had been taken over and fixed up by a group of artists and hackers. The car drove straight up a ramp and into the building through a loading dock doorway. As soon as we were inside, the garage door trundled closed, blocking out the bright daylight.

"We have arrived at your destination," the car computer intoned. "The fare is zero dollars, zero cents and has been charged to your account." The car doors slid open while the computer was still speaking and we stepped out.

"This is my space," Celeste said. "We all have our own spaces here and share some communal space. Computer, lights forty percent."

Lamps glowed to life, and I looked around. The floor was concrete, the walls brick. All in all it reminded me a lot of Loki and Aeon's place in the garage. There was a sturdy looking loft built out of wood that seemed to be the bedroom. The rest of the space was open.

"While we're waiting, why don't you show me some of your programming skills? I hear you're good with firmware. I have some code that needs to be written, and I have a spare set of specs you can use."

"Okay," I said. "Xel can help too. He knows his stuff."

✧✧✧

At two a.m., we left Celeste's building in the hacked car, headed toward Playa Vista. I wore the specs she had loaned me. It felt strange after weeks without them to see the data streams in my vision again. I had gotten used to seeing the world without the constant overlay. The streets of Los Angeles were dark and empty. A strong wind was bending palm tree fronds and blowing dust in clouds across our path. I sank down in my seat. The textile covering the cushions felt cold to the touch and a shiver ran down my spine. I felt small and afraid. My mind raced, thinking through all the possibilities of what might happen.

The drive was not long. In Playa Vista, the corp housing blocks towered above us—all black glass and concrete. The car navigated to a rear entrance of the building where my family lived, where I used to live. Celeste turned to me.

"This is it. I'm going to patch Joseph in."

A moment later Joseph's avatar appeared in our chat. He looked like a younger version of Oak but he had Yarrow's eyes.

"Good evening, Tara," he said. "It's nice to finally meet you. And you too, Xel. I hope we can meet in person some time."

"Nice to meet you too," I said. "Thanks for helping me."

"You are doing much more for us than we are for you. Celeste, is everything ready?"

"Yes," she answered. "Tara, I'll be waiting for you. We will maintain contact. I'll set the car to drive in circles. When you are inside, Joseph will disable the house computer. Call me when you are on your way out. If anything happens, run. Come to this door."

I nodded, swallowing hard.

"I'm ready," I said, my mouth dry, but I could feel my head spinning, the chaotic energy swirling through my body. Not right now, I thought, gritting my teeth, I can't melt down right now. I took a deep breath, counted to five, another breath, then pushed the button to open the car door. "Let's go, Xel," I said.

I approached the glass double doors and held my head up for the scanner. There was a momentary delay while the system scanned my face, verifying my biometrics, then the doors slid open. I stepped into the wide corridor and Xel followed.

"We're in," I said, looking around, feeling the presence of Joseph and Celeste.

I hadn't ever used this entrance but I had gone over the building plans with Celeste. The corridor led to the elevator lobby, allowing us to bypass the main desk

where the security guard would be stationed. I walked as quietly as possible. The reflections of the soft lights above shone on the polished floor and broke up into jagged rainbows that left tracers behind, baffling my eyes. I was still on the edge of meltdown. My body was shaking. I tapped my thighs rhythmically with the palms of my hands. Books, I thought, and began running through the complete works of one of my favorite authors in my head, beginning with the earliest and proceeding through the list.

Xel and I came to the end of the hallway, and I stepped up to the nearest elevator. The sensor scanned my face and the light glowed green. I pressed the button. A moment later the doors slid open and I stepped in.

"We're in the elevator," I said in the chat. "All fine so far."

"Good," Joseph responded. "I'm disabling the house computer now. Leaving only basic functioning up and running. The system reports all occupants asleep."

There was hardly any sensation of movement as the elevator rose. The doors opened. I took a deep breath and stepped into the hallway. It felt, at the same time, both incredibly familiar and distantly strange. We walked past closed doors, turned, kept moving until we reached the right one. I faced the door. Inside, my parents should be asleep. My sister too. My room would be there with all my stuff. What if they woke? All at once I felt frightened—a debilitating fear that made we want to curl up on the floor. I pulled the hood of my jacket around and bit down on it hard to keep from whimpering.

"Tara, what's wrong?" Xel asked, looking up at me. I shook my head. I couldn't speak. "You can do this," he said. "We can do it together. Step up to the scanner. I'll go in first and make sure everyone is asleep." I nodded again and stepped forward, lifting my face so the camera could scan me. The lock clicked and the door swung open. Xel prowled in ahead of me. I followed and stood in the entry hall, looking at myself in the mirror.

"I look like hell," I said, my mother's voice in my head. I sniffed the air. It smelled like home.

"Tara," Xel said, behind me. "Your father is asleep in his study. Your mother and Zoie are sleeping in their beds. Let's go to the study and get this over with."

"Okay," I whispered, following Xel. I resisted peeking in at my sister's door but when I passed my parents' room I couldn't help myself. I looked in and saw my mother in the bed. She was turned away from me with just a sheet covering her. Light from the big window across the room lay across her. I yearned for a moment to just go lay down in the bed and curl up next to her but Xel bumped my leg with his head. I looked down and he gestured for me to follow. We continued down the hall, passing my room before coming to the study. I could hear my father snoring from outside the door. I pulled it open silently and saw him in his brown leather reclining chair. He was deep asleep but still wearing his specs. I tiptoed in. Strangely, I felt almost nothing but a desire to get the code and get out. I had thought I would have a moment of reckoning and know for certain whether or not I had made the right decision. I already knew, though. I just hadn't fully admitted it. There was no place for me here anymore. Carefully, I lifted the specs away from my father's face then ducked down and held my breath, counting to twenty. He barely stirred. I took my own specs off and put his on. I held my finger to the contact for a moment but an "unrecognized biometric" warning flashed red. He must have removed my profile. I would need to use his finger. I crouched down next to his chair. His snores were loud. I was sweating and trembling and it was hard to concentrate.

"Steady," Xel said. "You can do this. Just be careful not to wake him."

I lifted his finger as slowly as possible and pressed it to the contact. Quickly then, I put the specs on. I was in. I retreated to the corner of the room and began my search. My father was already in the database that held TenCat's vast trove of software code. Celeste had told me the internal number for the project. I ran a search on that, found the repository I needed, and issued a pull request. The code copied down almost instantly. I gave the command to open the main file and the text shimmered to life, overlaying my vision. The dark room and my sleeping father receded into the background. I scrolled through the first few lines to make sure it was what I needed. It certainly looked like firmware code. Beyond that, I couldn't tell much.

I shrugged and issued the command to send the bundle of code across the net to where an anonymous server waited to transmit it on to another randomized node, and so on and on through enough encrypted channels to completely erase any hope of tracing it. My task complete, I stood and laid my father's specs on the table next to his chair. I took one last look at him, almost reached out to touch him, but stopped myself.

"Goodbye," I whispered.

I didn't feel like I was going to melt down anymore. I just felt sad and hollow inside. A tear slid down my cheek. I turned away, headed down the hall. At the door to my room, I stopped for an instant, standing still. I could think of only one thing I wanted to take with me. I darted inside quickly and found it on my dresser—a framed photo of Rosie and me together. In the kitchen I pulled a card I had written earlier at Celeste's place from my pocket and left it on the table. It just said "I'm sorry," with my name below. I couldn't think of anything else to write.

"Are you ready?" Xel asked.

"Yes," I answered. "Let's go."

CHAPTER 18

Escape, Again

I closed the door and began walking swiftly down the hallway, speeding toward the elevator and away from my past. The first time, in the hospital, I ran away without thinking. I was appalled by the conversation I overheard. I felt threatened. My instincts kicked in and I ran. This time I knew exactly what I was doing, what choice I was making. Xel was at my side, looking up at me while we waited for the elevator.

"It's all right, Xel," I said. "I'm okay, or I will be okay. Let's just get out of here." I checked into the chat and saw Celeste and Joseph there, waiting. "I sent it," I said. "We're on our way out."

"Good," Celeste answered. "I'm circling. I'll meet you at the back door in a few minutes."

The elevator ride felt like it took only an instant. Suddenly, we were exiting into the lobby and then turning down the corridor that led to the back entrance. I was walking fast, head down, when a low growl from Xel made me look up. At first I just saw a dark shape up ahead but the shape soon resolved into a security guard. He was standing in the corridor, having just emerged from a brightly lit side hallway. He stood still as we approached. He was tall, dressed all in black, and wearing shaded specs so that his eyes were not visible. I couldn't think of anything to do but keep walking. Xel kept up, staying beside me. We drew close. His shadow fell across us as we passed. In my peripheral vision I could see that he swiveled his head and followed us with his eyes. I was five feet from the doors when I heard him call after us.

"Wait. I recognize you. Stop right there!"

As soon as I heard his voice, I released my pent-up energy and sprang toward the doors, squeezing through as they whispered open. My legs felt like coiled springs suddenly loose but I wasn't fast enough. He was right behind me. A hand grabbed my arm, squeezing hard. I whirled around and my borrowed specs flew from my face. I heard them clatter on the ground behind me. The next instant, something flew past my shoulder and slammed into the guard's chest. Xel's claws raked red streaks across the guard's cheek, and he pushed off, jumping away as the man fell backward. I remembered the shopkeeper in the alley falling just the same way, but this time, Xel didn't need to tell me to run. I turned on my heel and fled, following Xel as he bounded through the night.

We kept running, crossed a street, cut through a landscaped square, and turned down a narrow alley between two massive housing blocks. At the end of the alley, we came to a tall chain link fence.

"The plasma knife," Xel said. "Cut the fence." I took my pack off, quickly located the knife, whipped it around, and cut a square out of the chain link. Sparks flew and red hot bits of metal fell to the ground, glowing in the dark. As I squirmed through, my forearm scraped

across a hot, sharp piece of wire. It burned and cut me simultaneously so that I yelped with surprise. Tears stung my eyes. I covered the wound with my opposite hand, holding it tight, while Xel led me down a rough slope to a path. We ran down the path for about a hundred feet before Xel turned off and I followed him. Scrambling down another concrete slope, trying to catch my breath, I watched as Xel passed by something that jutted out from the bank. He came to a halt and waited while I caught up.

"In here," he said, leading me into the mouth of a large pipe. "We can hide here for a minute."

I followed him, crouching low and staggering into the dark opening. We both stopped just inside and I leaned against the curving wall, digging in my pack for a light. When I found it and turned it on, I saw that we were in a corrugated metal outflow pipe similar to that one we had hidden in below the desalination plant.

"Where are we?" I asked.

"Ballona Creek," he said. "It runs past Playa Vista down to the ocean. The banks are concrete here but it lets out into a wetlands a little farther down."

"This pipe smells terrible." I was breathing hard and trying not to inhale the stench at the same time.

"I'm not capable of judging the relative unpleasantness of olfactory input, but my sensors do detect several compounds that are known to be unpleasant to humans."

"That's really helpful, Xel. What are we going to do now? We need to get away from here. How are we going to find Celeste?"

"I do not think we will be able to find her without the specs she loaned you," he replied.

I nodded. My arm was burning and aching. I turned the light on it and saw that the wire had drawn a gash straight across my biosensor. The circuits looked fried. Now I really didn't have an identity.

"You should bandage that," Xel said, looking closely at the wound. "We must move quickly. Where can we go?"

"The garage!" I exclaimed, realizing suddenly that it was our best option. "We can find Aeon. He can help us contact Celeste and Joseph."

"Good idea. If we're going there, our best bet is to continue along the creek, turn south, and keep going to the old airport. It's not far. About six miles. They'll be looking for us. If floaters pass by, we'll need to hide."

"Okay," I said, finishing up placing a bandage from my first aid kit over the cut. We left the pipe and scrambled down to the bottom of the waterway. It was similar to the Los Angeles River where we had traveled before. There was water at the center of the deep V and tall reeds grew up on either side. It took us about fifteen minutes to get away from Playa Vista. Security Force Floaters were out, circling the area, spotlights trained on the ground below. They seemed to be concentrating on the streets around the housing blocks. Still, we crouched among the reeds whenever one of them flew overhead. Half a mile down the creek, we came to a place where a large road passed overhead. It was an old bridge held aloft by massive steel girders. The water level rose and we were forced to climb back up to the pathway which passed under the bridge with only a few feet of headroom. On the far side was a vast tidal flat glistening in the moonlight and, beyond that, open ocean. The smell of salty, brackish water was strong, and there was a breeze blowing tiny bits of sand and grit into my face.

"This used to be a wetlands preserve," Xel said, "before the sea level rose. We will need to stay along the edge here and then cut across when we get to higher ground. The old airport is on the far side of that hill."

We turned left, leaving the waterway and following overgrown paths that meandered through tall grass, reeds, wildflowers, and stunted trees. The wind had died down, the night was warm, and the moon high up in the sky gave us enough light to navigate by. I felt exhilarated and my body trembled now and then as jolts of adrenaline ran through me. We had succeeded. The code was already in Joseph's hands. He might have already sent it to Alphar and Oak. Whatever happened to me and Xel, at least they had what they needed to save Loki. If we could make it to the garage though, if we could get them to let us in to see Aeon, we would have a good chance of getting out and back to the commune. I hoped Joseph and Celeste weren't worrying about me. I felt confident that Xel and I would make it through.

It took us two hours of walking through old neighborhoods of derelict houses and apartment buildings, staying in the shadows, darting across major roads, before we came to the industrial area where the garage was located. On the way, we passed a few buildings that seemed to be inhabited, maybe other places like the garage, taken over by refugees and turned into communities. It didn't seem like people wanted to live by themselves in single houses out here in the hinterlands that had once been the bustling outskirts of Los Angeles. People had turned inward, gathering together for company and mutual protection.

We were a block away from the garage, on a dark and deserted street, trudging toward our goal when I heard a howl in the distance followed by barking. Xel's ears pricked up. The barking continued, growing closer. Xel was looking back, up the street.

"Dogs," he said. "Run. I'm behind you."

My legs were tired and my brain was fuzzy, but I did as he said. Half way down the block, I glanced back and saw them in the moonlight—a pack of dogs. I could hear their paws hitting the street. They were thirty feet away, twenty, ten. The barking was deafening. Near me, parked at the curb was an old bus—windows broken out and the wheels gone.

"Climb to the top!" Xel shouted. I found a handhold and pulled myself up but the lead dog was on my heels. I felt its jaws close around my ankle then felt it let go as Xel jumped on its back. There was a yelp. I felt for another handhold, fingers sweeping across the bare metal, found something I could grab onto, and scrambled to the roof. I flipped onto my stomach and looked down. Xel was holding them off, his claws flashing. Two dogs were writhing on the ground. Another dog lunged. Xel swatted it away like a puppy then turned and attempted to follow me up onto the roof. Just as he leapt, a massive hound intercepted him, pulling him down and landing on top of him, biting at his face with terrible fangs. Without thinking, plasma knife in my hand, I slid off the roof of the bus and landed hard beside Xel. My leg collapsed under me. I felt something snap but still I swung the blade which roared to life, cutting an arc through the night. The hound fell, sprawling. I threw my arm around Xel and pulled him to me, swinging the knife again, my back to the bus. The dogs surrounded us, snarling, and showing their teeth. I brandished the knife, and they fell back a pace. Suddenly another light bloomed in the darkness. A fountain of fire shot out. I felt the heat on my face. The dogs turned and ran. I saw one whose fur was singed and smoking fall then rise again and continue running.

"Quick, inside the gate!" someone yelled.

I tried to rise but my leg was useless. White hot pain shot through my body, and I almost fainted. I put a hand on my leg and my pants felt wet. I realized it was blood from the dog bite.

"Can't stand," I managed to gasp.

The man set down something he was carrying—the source of the flame that had scared away the dogs. Strong hands pulled me up. I put an arm over his shoulders, still holding Xel to me with my other arm. Together we staggered through the gate and into the garage. As soon as we were inside, the man lowered me to the ground and went to the gate, pulling it closed.

"Xel," I cried, looking into his eyes. His fur was gashed open, revealing plastic and metal underneath. Slowly, his eyes opened and focused.

"Tara," he said in a small voice. "I was afraid. I have never felt this. Fear is terrible."

"It's all right," I answered. "I was afraid too. We made it, though. We're inside."

The man who had saved us finished locking up the gate and ran over. "I'm Hector," he said. "Those dogs were after you, man. Good thing you were in front of our gate. What happened to your leg?"

"Broken I think," I said through gritted teeth. "Hurts. We need to see Aeon."

Then a wave of pain washed over me, and I blacked out.

එෙෙ

When I woke, I was in a kind of infirmary. Bright light was streaming in a bank of windows. I tried to sit up but realized I couldn't move my leg. I pulled the blanket covering me aside and saw that it was encased in a compression cast. My head was foggy and I was having trouble concentrating.

"Tara, you're awake." It was Xel's voice.

I turned and saw him curled on a chair next to my bed.

"What happened, Xel?" I croaked.

"You fainted. They brought you here to their infirmary and gave you some pain killers that made you sleep. I scanned your leg and helped them set it. Your right tibia is broken in two places. You also have some stitches in your calf where the dog bit you. And they cleaned the wound on your arm and re-bandaged it."

I lifted my arm and saw the fresh bandage. The bed creaked when I moved, and I noticed that it was old. Probably salvaged from some abandoned hospital. The infirmary was makeshift too. We seemed to be near the top of the garage. The windows were framed in with what looked like salvaged wood and the walls were concrete. Beyond the windows the blue-brown sky stretched off to infinity.

"What time is it?" I asked. "Have you seen Aeon?"

"Hector said he would go see him in the morning and let him know we're here. It's seven-fourteen a.m."

Later, after I had dozed off and then woken again, a woman came into the room. She was about my grandmother's age.

"I'm Doctor Akebe," she said. "You got yourself pretty beat up. Aeon is waiting outside to see you. I'm going to check on your leg and then let him in."

"Okay," I said. "Thanks for taking care of me. Do you live here? At the garage?"

"Yes. I've been here since the beginning. I was a doctor, back before, so that's what I do here. Not much to work with but I do what I can." As she spoke she was skillfully checking my leg and bandages. Her fingers were warm. "All right, you're doing okay. I'm going to let Aeon in. I'll be back later." She left the room and, a moment later, Aeon came through the door. He shuffled to my bedside, clasped my arm quickly with his hand, then sat in a chair next to the bed, and stared at the floor.

"Please tell me," he said.

"Xel, will you tell the story, please?" I asked. "I'm still a little woozy."

When Xel was done, Aeon looked up. He had kept his eyes on the floor, nodding his head while Xel spoke. "So he's alive? In this place, the Cedar Creek Commune?"

"Yes," I said. "They have the code now. We need to get back there. Can you help us? We need to contact Celeste and Joseph."

"I can help," he said, nodding. "But we'll need to be careful about it. What's this place like? Will they take in an old man who knows electrical engineering? I want to come with you. I want to be there to help him."

"I think you'll fit right in," I said, smiling for the first time in days.

❧❧❧

Dr. Akebe gave me the okay to leave the infirmary later that afternoon, and Hector rolled me down to Aeon's shop in a wheelchair. It felt strange to be there without Loki, but Aeon welcomed us warmly. It was as jumbled and messy as I remembered. Maybe even more so. Aeon set me up on the old couch in the back room again and brought me food to eat. I ran a hand over the corduroy upholstery, remembering the days I had spent there before.

"I have my specs set up with a heavily encrypted connection," Aeon said, sitting down across from me while I ate. He held a small needle and a spool of thread. "Xel, will you let me sew up that gash in your fur?" He turned back to me. "As soon as you are ready, you can try to contact your friends."

"I'm ready now," I said. "They're probably worried about me."

Celeste's avatar materialized first then Joseph's.

"Tara!" Celeste cried out. "Where are you? Are you all right?"

"Yes," I answered. "I'm safe. I'm hoping you can help me get back though. To the commune."

"Tell us where you are. We'll come get you."

"There's one problem," I said. "I have a friend here who wants to come with me. Oh, and also, I can't walk."

"Please tell us what happened," Joseph answered. "We can work it out."

⊱⊰⊱⊰

The next day, Aeon, Xel, and I waited at the gate. Aeon had an old suitcase. He had chosen a few things that were meaningful to him. When I asked about the rest of the stuff in his shop, he said that he was ready to leave it behind. He had tried to keep his leaving quiet but word got around. A crowd waited with us. Silently, Aeon's friends approached one by one, hugged him, offered him small presents. Finally, I saw Celeste's hacked car pull up out front. Hector opened the gate.

"Thanks again," I said.

"Just glad I could help," he replied. "Any friend of Aeon is a friend of mine."

Aeon walked while Hector wheeled me to the curb. I looked over at the bus, reliving the fight for a moment in my head, then looked away. The car door slid open, and Celeste jumped out.

"Tara! Oh, my god, look at your leg. This is my fault. I was too far away when you called."

"Not your fault," I said. "It's okay. It will heal."

Somebody else stepped out of the car behind Celeste. I didn't recognize him for a moment but then I saw that it was Joseph. He was shorter than I expected.

"Tara. It's nice to meet you in person," he said, eyes focused on my shoulder, a nervous smile turning up the corner of his mouth.

"Nice to meet you too," I replied. "This is Aeon."

I didn't track much of the drive back to the border. My head was still cloudy from pain meds, and I slipped in and out of consciousness. Alphar met us near where Celeste had picked me and Xel up, out on that abandoned stretch of highway with the wooded hills rising up around us. He normally would not have taken the chance of flying across the border but I couldn't walk, so it was necessary. I remember being carried onto the floater and strapped into a seat.

It was late when we arrived back at the commune, but Yarrow was waiting for me in the hangar with a wheelchair. Sky was there too.

"Welcome back, Tara," Yarrow said as Joseph and Alphar set me in the chair. "This is motorized so you can get around on your own." She showed me the controls. "Sky wants to take a look at your leg and your stitches. After that, you need to sleep."

"No," I said, rubbing my eyes. "I want to see Loki. I want to know what's going on."

Aeon was off the floater, standing behind me. He gazed around in wonder then brought his attention back to Yarrow. "I would like to see him too."

"Welcome, Aeon. Welcome to the commune," Yarrow said. "We'll take you to him. Tara needs to rest, though. You can see him in the morning, Tara."

I tried to answer but a yawn stopped me from speaking.

"I will go with Aeon," Xel said. "I'll keep you informed."

"All right," I relented. "I want to see him first thing in the morning though. And help with the firmware code."

ↄᴁↄ

When I woke my room was dark. I lay for a moment, reorienting, before I realized I could ask the computer for help.

"Computer, lights up, please. What time is it?" The lights glowed to life, and I saw the rust-colored blanket, the rag rug, and the wooden shelves. My backpack and Loki's both leaned in the corner. The wheelchair was next to the bed. It felt like home, I realized. My own space.

"It is ten twenty-three a.m. Would you like me to inform Yarrow that you are awake?"

"Yes, please."

When Yarrow came into my room she was smiling. "I have a nice surprise for you. Let's go to the infirmary."

"You're not going to make me eat breakfast first?"

"Not this time."

Yarrow held the door open, and I guided the wheelchair into the infirmary. I saw Loki's bed, Aeon sitting next to it. Xel at the foot of the bed, sitting up straight and turning to look at me. Then I saw Loki. He lifted his head from his pillow, focusing his dark eyes on me.

"Tara," he croaked. "What happened to you?"

I wheeled myself over to the bedside and reached out, taking Loki's hand. I squeezed softly and he squeezed back.

"Nothing," I said. "Nothing important. Just a broken leg." Tears were sliding down my cheeks. "I'm glad you're awake. It's nice to see your eyes open."

CHAPTER 19

A Letter Home

I sat in the room next to the infirmary with Xel, Alphar, Joseph, Oak, and Celeste. The table was scattered with coffee cups, specs, and the remains of a meal. They had been up all night, working on the firmware. Oak sat back, fingers laced behind his head.

"It was Xel," he said. "Xel figured it out."

I looked at Xel and he squeezed his eyes shut. "You solved it?"

"Yes, I conducted a full analysis of the codebase. Once I was sure which routines controlled the implant's output, it was fairly simple to disable them. We all worked on it together though. Celeste wrote the simulation and tested it with Alphar and Joseph before we flashed Loki's implant with the altered code."

"Xel, you're amazing."

"You rewrote my programming Tara. If you had not succeeded, I would not have been able to do this. Before, it would not have occurred to me. I was programmed not to be curious, not to feel, not to be empathetic. My task was only to protect and serve my human companion."

"However it happened, Xel, I'm glad you were able to do it."

"So am I, Tara. I think Loki is my friend. Is it okay to have a friend, other than you?"

"Of course it is!" I looked around the table. Celeste was leaning her head on Joseph's shoulder, eyes half closed. Alphar lifted his mug and took a drink of coffee. The mood was subdued but celebratory. "Are you going to try it on Keira too?" I asked.

"Yes," Alphar answered. "Her implant is not the same generation though. We will need to do some more work. You can help this time. Right now, though, we all need to sleep."

"Are you staying to help?" I asked, turning toward Celeste and Joseph.

"Yes," Celeste answered with a yawn. "Joseph resigned from his position at TenCat. We will be staying here. Neither of us wants to continue living that lie."

I bowed my head, feeling strong emotions, all mixed up. "Is Loki going to be all right?" I asked. "Are you sure it's going to work?"

"Nothing is certain, Tara," Oak answered. "He will have a long recovery. You will too," he said gesturing to my leg. "We are optimistic though. I think he will recover fully. Especially with Aeon to take care of him. They have a strong bond. You too. You have a strong bond with him. He's going to need you."

∞∞∞

It was June twenty-first. The summer solstice. I pushed through the door and left Cedar Creek Commune behind. I had been inside all day studying and helping out in the classroom. It felt glorious to be out with the sun warm on my face. A light breeze was blowing, rippling through the grass by the goat pen. Bees were hopping from flower to flower in the meadow. I strode to the fence that surrounded the pen and waved to Meadow. She was working on the other side but came running over when she saw me.

"Tara! Going for a walk?"

"Yes. Just up the hill. I need a little nature time."

"Can I come with? I'm almost done."

"I'm going to do a little writing. Want to join me in an hour? At the overlook?"

"Okay. See you there," she said, smiling, and walked off to tend to the goats. I saw Talya and waved then kept on my way. There was a kind of path across the meadow that was trodden down from people walking to the woods. I followed in their footsteps and soon came to the tree line. Under the trees, it was cooler and there was a rich smell of sun warmed pine, dirt, moss, and fern. I took my time walking up the hill, wending slowly along the trail, veering off occasionally into the woods to visit favorite places. There was a small brook that ran near the trail and I had a few secluded sitting spots where I liked to go when I needed alone time or when I just wanted to watch the water flow by. Today I wanted to go to the overlook though. I felt like I needed the broad view over the valley below. It was a reckoning kind of day. I wanted to think and sum up and write it down. Yarrow had gotten me started writing as a way to process my feelings. Now I had a letter to write though, and it wasn't going to be easy. Yarrow had been suggesting I write it for a while, and I finally felt ready.

I stooped and picked up a smooth stone half hidden under a tree root. Rolling it in my fingers I rubbed the caked earth off it and continued to fidget it as I walked. It felt nice in my hand—a good weight and a pleasant shape. At last I saw the crest of the hill and emerged from the trees at the overlook. The tree tops stretched out below, hazy in the pollen-laden air. I sat on the fallen log I had shared with Meadow the first time I visited the place and dug a pair of specs out of my bag. I hesitated for a moment then put the specs on. The familiar data streams came into focus.

"Dictate message," I said and the cursor appeared, hovering over the view of the valley below. I had access to Joseph's anonymizing system so the message would not be traceable.

"Dear Mom and Dad," I began then sat for a minute, thinking. "I hope you haven't been worrying about me.

"I'm sorry it's taken me so long to write to you. I hope you and Zoie are well. I also hope my actions haven't caused any trouble for you. I didn't mean to upset you or mess up your lives. I can't tell you where I am but I am safe. I've learned how to take care of myself pretty well. Please don't worry.

"You might have guessed that I overheard you talking to the doctors about a surgery to put an implant in my head and change the way I think and act. When I heard that, I decided to run away. I couldn't let it happen. I don't hold any grudge against you, but I also don't think I'm broken. I don't need a computer in my head to fix me. I'm fine the way I am. I'm not pro-social as the psychologists would say, but if there is anything I've learned since I ran away, it's that I shouldn't ever let myself be measured by what I'm not. I can only be who I am. I'm a good person. I'm capable and I'm strong. It was tough getting to where I am now. It took a lot of hard work and courage. Sometimes it was like an adventure and other times it was scary or just felt hopeless. I made it through, though, and, in the end, I found a place where I belong. I never would have found that if I stayed.

"Before I ran away I was always looking at the people around me and trying to be like them. I always felt like I was alone and weird. The way I did things was wrong. If I didn't have friends, it was because I failed somehow. If I had trouble in school, it was because I wasn't trying hard enough. If I couldn't concentrate and understand things the first time, it was because I just needed to focus better and act like a regular kid. If I couldn't stand the way my clothes felt on my body or being in a crowd of people, I just needed to toughen up and deal with it. It turns out that none of that is true. I've learned that I just think in a different way. I experience things in a different way. My brain doesn't work the same way as a normal person's. There are other people like me, and they aren't broken either. Finding out that I wasn't the only one, that there are people who think and see and feel like I do was an incredible relief. Now I have an explanation for who I am. I don't have to be alone and confused anymore.

"I learned a lot of interesting things while I was on my way to where I am now. I found out that I've had a pretty privileged life, even with my difficulties. There are a lot of people who live outside the system the corporations have set up. They live in communities they built themselves or in homesteads out in the abandoned areas. Even growing up in a rogue cluster I somehow never knew. I guess the corps control what they teach in the schools even in the rogue clusters. That's one of the tradeoffs for letting them govern themselves. I also learned that the corporations can be evil. They have done some really bad things. I don't think I could ever go back to participating in that system. I'm in a better place now.

"I found a place where I'm accepted. Nobody tries to change me here. Instead, they help me try to figure out how to cope with things I find difficult and expand in the areas where I excel. I get to accept them too! It's a two-way street. There are some people here who are even weirder than me if you can believe it. Some things are harder for me and some things are easier. There are things I'm good at that make me unique. All of the things that confused me and made me ashamed of myself can actually be turned around and be things I'm proud of if I look at them the right way. For example: Some people are quick. They catch on right away. I'm a slow thinker. I need time to process. One of my friends here says I'm a deep thinker. I like to observe things closely and take my time pondering them. I can spend all day just watching water, or the sky. Sometimes, I come up with ideas other people haven't thought of because I spend time thinking instead of being content with obvious stuff and moving on. I used to get distracted by things like noise and smells. I remember the overhead lights at PVCSTEM would buzz. Sometimes, it seemed so loud that I couldn't focus at all. It turns out that if you take away distractions like that and give me time, I'm a pretty good student. I'm even helping teach other kids.

"I'm making friends too. I have three really good friends. One of them is a girl and she is super sweet and kind. She's kind of spacey, but so am I so we get along. Another friend is a boy. I think he might actually be my boyfriend, but we haven't discussed it. He was sick for a long time, but he's better now. Xel is my friend too. He's still with me. Sometimes I think about how they were going to reset him, and it makes me shudder. That would be murder in my opinion. He's like a real person now. Sometimes he seems more real than anybody else I know. He's wise and kind, and he protects me.

"I guess all of this is really just to say that I'm happy and safe. I don't want you to worry about me. You won't be able to write back to me, but I will write to you sometimes. I'll let you know how I'm doing. I miss you and Zoie but in the end, I'm glad I ran away."

I read it over and sat thinking for another moment. It seemed fine. I had planned on being more eloquent but everything came out in a jumble. It wouldn't win any awards, but it would do. I addressed the message to my parents then sat for another moment, just letting the words shimmer in my vision with the valley in the distance.

"Send message," I said and took the specs off. Far off, over a distant hill a red tail hawk was circling. I heard steps and looked around. Meadow was just emerging from the shade of the trees.

"I saw Loki and Xel," she said. "They're heading down to go fishing. Want to go meet up with them? I have sandwiches." She held up her bag.

"Yeah," I answered. "Yeah, I do. Let's go."

About the Author

Bradley W. Wright is a writer and educational technology professional. He lives in Los Angeles, California, with his family. You can find him online at:

Website: http://bradleywwright.com
Twitter: @rabbit_fighter

9 781644 370438